# the thief

by

## megan whalen turner

greenwillow books
new york

Library of Congress Cataloging-in-Publication Data
Turner, Megan Whalen.
    The thief / by Megan Whalen Turner.
        p.    cm.
    Summary: Gen flaunts his ingenuity as a thief
and relishes the adventure which takes him to
a remote temple of the gods where he will
attempt to steal a precious stone.
    ISBN 0-688-14627-9
    [1. Robbers and outlaws—Fiction.
2. Adventure and adventurers—Fiction.]
I. Title.
PZ7.T85565Th    1996
[Fic]—dc20
95-41040    CIP    AC

for sandy passarelli

# chapter 1

*I* DIDN'T KNOW HOW LONG I had been in the king's prison. The days were all the same, except that as each one passed, I was dirtier than before. Every morning the light in the cell changed from the wavering orange of the lamp in the sconce outside my door to the dim but even glow of the sun falling into the prison's central courtyard. In the evening, as the sunlight faded, I reassured myself that I was one day closer to getting out. To pass time, I concentrated on pleasant memories, laying them out in order and examining them carefully. I reviewed over and over the plans that had seemed so straightforward before I arrived in jail, and I swore to myself and every god I knew that if I got out alive, I would never never never take any risks that were so abysmally stupid again.

I was thinner than I had been when I was first arrested. The large iron ring around my waist had grown loose, but not loose enough to fit over the bones of my hips. Few prisoners wore chains in their cells, only those that the king particularly disliked: counts or dukes or the minister of the exchequer when he told the king there wasn't any more money to spend. I was certainly none of those things, but I suppose it's safe to say that the king disliked me. Even if he didn't remember my name or whether I was as common as dirt, he didn't want me slipping away. So I had chains on my ankles as well as the iron belt around my waist and an entirely useless set of chains locked around my wrists. At first I pulled the cuffs off my wrists, but since I sometimes had to force them back on quickly, my wrists started to be rubbed raw. After a while it was less painful just to leave the manacles on. To take my mind off my daydreams, I practiced moving around the cell without clanking.

I had enough chain to allow me to pace in an arc from a front corner of the cell out to the center of the room and back to the rear corner. My bed was there at the back, a bench made of stone with a thin bag of sawdust on top. Beside it was the chamber pot. There was nothing else in the cell except myself and the chain and, twice a day, food.

The cell door was a gate of bars. The guards looked in at me as they passed on their rounds, a tribute to my reputation. As part of my plans for greatness, I had bragged without shame about my skills in every wine store in the city. I had wanted everyone to know that I was the finest thief since mortal men were made, and I must have come close to accomplishing the goal. Huge crowds had gathered for my trial. Most of the guards in the prison had turned out to see me after my arrest, and I was endlessly chained to my bed when other prisoners were sometimes allowed the freedom and sunshine of the prison's courtyard.

There was one guard who always seemed to catch me with my head in my hands, and he always laughed.

"What?" he would say. "Haven't you escaped yet?"

Every time he laughed, I spat insults at him. It was not politic, but as always, I couldn't keep an insult in when it wanted to come out. Whatever I said, the guard laughed more.

I ached with cold. It had been early in the spring when I'd been arrested and dragged out of the Shade Oak Wineshop. Outside the prison walls the summer's heat must have dried out the city and driven everyone indoors for afternoon naps, but the prison cells got no direct sun, and they were as damp and cold as when I had first arrived. I spent hours dreaming of the sunshine, the way it soaked into the city walls and made the yellow stones hot to lean on hours after the day had ended, the way it dried out water spills and the rare libations to the gods still occasionally poured into the dust outside the wineshops.

Sometimes I moved as far as my chains would let me and looked through the bars of my cell door and across the deep gallery that shaded the prison cells at the sunlight falling into the courtyard. The prison was two stories of cells stacked one on top of the other; I was in the upper level. Each cell opened onto the gallery, and the gallery was separated from the courtyard by stone pillars. There were no windows in the outside walls, which were three or four feet thick, built of massive stones that ten men together couldn't have shifted. Legends said that the old gods had stacked them together in a day.

The prison was visible from almost anywhere in the city because the city was built on a hill and the prison was at the summit. The only other building there was the king's home, his megaron. There had also been a temple to the old gods once, but it had been destroyed, and the basilica to the new gods was built farther down the hill. Once the king's home had been a true megaron, one room, with a throne and a hearth, and the prison had been the agora, where citizens met and merchants hawked their jumble. The individual cells had been stalls of clothes or wine or candles or jewelry imported from the islands. Prominent citizens used to stand on the stone blocks in the courtyard to make speeches.

Then the invaders had come with their longboats and their own ideas of commerce; they did their trading in open markets next to their ships. They had taken over the king's megaron for their governor and used the solid stone building of the agora as a prison. Prominent citizens ended up chained to the blocks, instead of standing on them.

The old invaders were pushed out by new invaders, and in time Sounis revolted and had her own king again. Still, people did their trading down by the waterfront; it had become habit, and the new king continued to use the agora as a prison. It was useful to him, as he was no relation to any of the families that had ruled the city in the past. By the time I ended up there, most people in the city had forgotten the prison was ever anything but a holding pen for those who failed to pay their taxes and other criminals.

I was lying on my back in my cell, with my feet in the air, wrapped in the chain that led from my waist to a ring high in the wall. It was late at night, the sun had been gone for hours, and the prison was lit by burning lamps. I was weighing the merits of clean clothes versus better food and not paying attention to the tramp of feet outside my cell. There was an iron door that led from the prison into a guardroom at the narrow end of the building. The guards passed through it many times a day. If I heard the door banging, I no longer took any notice of it, so I was unprepared when lamplight, concentrated by a lens, flared into my cell. I wanted to look lithe and graceful and perhaps feral as I unwrapped my feet and sat up. Caught by surprise and nearly blind, I was clumsy and would have fallen off the stone bunk if the chain had not still been wrapped around one foot.

"This is the right one?"

No wonder the voice sounded surprised. I levered myself upright and blinked into the lamplight, unable to see much. The guard reassured someone that this indeed was the prisoner he wanted.

"All right. Take him out."

The guard said, "Yes, magus," as he unlocked the barred gate, so I knew who it was at my door late at night. One of the king's most powerful advisors. In the days before the invaders came, the king's magus was supposed to have been a sorcerer, but not even the most superstitious believed that anymore. A magus was a scholar. He read scrolls and books in every language and studied everything that had ever been written and things that had never been written as well. If the king needed to know how many shafts of grain grew on a particular acre of land, the magus could tell him. If the king wanted to know how many farmers would starve if he burned that acre of grain, the magus knew that, too. His knowledge, matched by his skills of persuasion, gave him the power to influence the king, and that made him a powerful figure at the court. He'd been at my trial. I had seen him sitting in a gallery behind the judges with one leg crossed over the other and his arms folded over his chest.

Once I had disentangled myself from the chains, the guards unlocked the rings on my feet, using a key as big as my thumb. They left the manacles on my wrists but released the chain that attached them to the waist ring. Then they hauled me to my feet and out of the cell. The magus looked me up and down and wrinkled his nose, probably at the smell.

He wanted to know my name.

I said, "Gen." He wasn't interested in the rest.

"Bring him along," he said as he turned his back on me and walked away. All of my own impulses to balance and move seemed to conflict with those of the guards, and I was jerked and jostled down the portico, just as graceful as a sick cat. We crossed through the guardroom to a door that led through the outer wall of prison to a flight of stone steps and a courtyard that lay between the prison and the south wing of the king's megaron. The megaron's walls rose four stories over our heads on three sides. The king's tiny stronghold had become a palace under the supervision of the invaders and an even larger palace since then. We crossed the courtyard, following a guard carrying a lantern, to a shorter flight of steps that led up to a door in the wall of the megaron)

On the other side of the door the white walls of a passageway reflected the light of so many lamps that it seemed as bright as day inside. I threw my head sideways and dragged one arm away from a guard in order to cover my eyes. The light felt solid, like spears that went through my head. Both guards stopped, and the one tried to grab my arm back, but I dragged it away again. The magus stopped to see what the noise was.

"Give him a moment to let his eyes adjust," he said.

It was going to take longer, but the minute helped. I blinked some of the tears out of my eyes, and we started down the passageway again. I kept my head down and my eyes nearly closed and didn't see much of the passageways at first. They had marble floors. The baseboards were painted with an occasional patch of lilies and a tortoise or resting bird. We went up a staircase where a painted pack of hunting dogs chased a lion around a corner to a door, where we stopped.

The magus knocked and went in. The guards, with some difficulty, navigated themselves and me through the narrow doorway. I looked around to see who had watched my clumsy entrance, but the room was empty.

I was excited. My blood rushed around like wine sloshing in a jar, but I was also deadly tired. The walk up the stairs had felt like a hike up a mountain. My knees wobbled, and I was glad to have the guards, graceless as they were, holding me at the elbows. When they let go, I was off-balance and had to swing my arms to keep from falling. My chains clanked.

"You can go," the magus said to the guards. "Come take him back in half an hour."

Half an hour? My hopes, which had been rising, fell a little. As the guards left, I looked around the room. It was small, with a desk and several comfortable chairs scattered around it. The magus stood next to the desk. The windows behind him should have looked out on the megaron's greater courtyard, but the tiny panes of glass only reflected the light of lamps burning inside. I looked again at the chairs. I picked the nicest one and sat in it. The magus stiffened. His eyebrows snapped down into a single line across the top of his face. They were dark, though most of his hair had gone to gray.

"Get up," he commanded.

I leaned farther into the feather pillows on the seat and back of the chair. It was almost as good as clean clothes, and I couldn't have gotten up if I had tried. My knees were weak, and my stomach was considering tossing up the little I had recently eaten. The chair back came to just behind my ears, so I rested my head back and looked up my nose at the magus, still standing by his desk.

The magus gave me a few moments to consider my position before he stepped over to the chair. He leaned down until his nose was just a few inches from mine. I hadn't seen his face before from this close. He had the high-bridged nose of most of the people in the city, but his eyes were a very light gray instead of brown. His forehead was covered by wrinkles brought on by a lot of sun and too much frowning. I was thinking that he must have done some sort of outdoor work before he started reading books when he spoke. I stopped thinking about his complexion and shifted my gaze back to his eyes.

"We might someday attain a relationship of mutual respect," he said softly. First, I thought, I will see gods walking the earth He went on. "For now I will have your obedience."

His ability to convey a world of threat in so few words was remarkable. I swallowed, and my hands shook a little where they lay on the arms of the chair. One link of chain clinked against another, but I still didn't try to get up. My legs wouldn't have lifted me. He must have realized this, and known also that he had made his point, because he stepped back to lean against the desk, and waved one hand in disgust.

"Never mind. Stay there for now. The seat will have to be cleaned."

I felt my face getting redder. It wasn't my fault that I stank. He should spend some months in the king's prison and then we'd see if he still smelled like old books and scented soap. He looked me over for several moments more and didn't seem impressed.

"I saw you at your trial," he said finally.

I didn't say that I'd noticed him there as well.

"You're thinner."

I shrugged.

"Tell me," said the magus, "have you found yourself reluctant to leave our hospitality? You said at your trial that not even the king's prison could hold you, and I rather expected you to be gone by now." He was enjoying himself.

I crossed my legs and settled deeper into the chair. He winced.

I said, "Some things take time."

"How true," said the magus. "How much time do you think it's going to take?"

Another half an hour, I thought, but I didn't say that either.

"I think it's going to take a long time," said the magus. "I think it could take the rest of your life. After all," he joked, "when you're dead, you certainly won't be in the king's prison, will you?"

"I suppose not." I didn't think he was funny.

"You boasted about a lot of things at your trial. Idle boasts, I suppose."

"I can steal anything."

"So you claimed. It was a wager to that effect that landed you in prison." He picked a pen nib off the desk beside him and turned it in his hands for a moment. "It is too bad for you that intelligence does not always attend gifts such as yours, and fortunate for me that it is not your intelligence I am interested in, but your skill. If you are as good as you say you are."

I repeated myself. "I can steal anything."

"Except yourself out of the king's prison?" the magus asked, lifting only one eyebrow this time.

I shrugged. I could do that, too, but it would take time. It might take a long time, and I wanted the king's magus to offer a faster way.

"Well, you've learned how to keep your mouth shut at least," said the magus. He pulled himself away from his desk and walked across the room. While his back was turned, I pushed the hair away from my eyes and took another quick look around the room. It was his study, but I already knew that. There were books and old scrolls in piles on the shelves. There was a scarred bench piled with amphoras and other clay containers. There were glass bottles as well. At the end of the room was a curtained alcove, and barely visible under the curtain was a pair of feet in leather boots. I turned back around in my chair with my stomach jumping.

"You could shorten the time without shortening your life," said the magus.

I looked up at him. I'd lost the thread of the conversation. In the moment it took me to recover it, I realized that he was now nervous himself. I relaxed in my seat. "Go on."

"I want you to steal something."

I smiled. "Do you want the king's seal? I can get it for you."

"If I were you," said the magus, "I'd stop bragging about that." His voice grated.

My smile grew. The gold ring with the engraved ruby had been in his safekeeping when I had stolen it away. Losing it, I was sure, had badly damaged his standing at the king's court. He glanced over my shoulder at the curtained alcove, and then he got to the point.

"There's something I want you to steal. Do this for me, and I'll see that you don't go back to prison. Fail to do this for me, and I will still make sure that you don't go back to prison."

Prisoners left the king's prison all the time. Masons, carpenters, blacksmiths, any skilled craftsmen could expect to finish their sentences working for the king's profit. Unskilled workers were collected several times a year and sent to the silver mines south of the city. They rarely returned, and other prisoners just disappeared.

It was clear enough what the magus had in mind, so I nodded. "What am I stealing?" That was all I cared about.

The magus dismissed the question. "You can find out the details later. What I need to know now is that you're capable." That I hadn't been overcome by disease, crippled, or starved beyond usefulness while in prison.

"I'm capable," I said. "But I have to know what I'm stealing."

"You'll be told. For now it isn't your business."

"What if I can't steal it?"

"I thought that you could steal anything," he taunted.

"Except myself out of the king's prison," I agreed.

"Don't try to be smart." The magus shook his head. "You don't pretend well." I opened my mouth to say something I shouldn't have, but he went on. "It will require some traveling to reach my object. There will be plenty of time for you to learn about it as we go."

I sat back in my chair, mollified and delighted. If I got out of the city of Sounis, no one would bring me back. The magus had to have known exactly what I was thinking because he leaned close over me again.

"Don't think that I am a fool."

He wasn't a fool, that much was true. But he didn't have my motivation. He leaned back against the desk, and I sat back in my chair thinking that the gods had listened to my prayers at last. Then I heard the rings on the top of the curtain behind me slide across their rod, and I remembered the two feet in the alcove. My stomach, which had settled a little, began to jump again.

The boots stamped across the room, and a hand came over the back of the chair in order to grab me by the hair. The owner of the hand lifted me up as he walked to the front of the chair and held me facing him. "Don't think that I am a fool either," he said.

He was short, just as his father had been, and stocky. His hair was a dark gold color and curled around his ears. It would have looked effeminate on anyone else. It probably endeared him to his mother when he was a child, but there was nothing endearing about him now. My hair was pulling free of my head, and I was standing on the tips of my toes to relieve the strain. I put both hands on top of his, tried to push the hand down, and found myself hanging entirely off the ground.

He dropped me. My legs folded under me, and I sat on the floor with a thump that jarred my entire body. I rubbed my head, trying to push the hair back into my scalp. When I looked up, the king was wiping his hand on the front of his clothes.

"Get up," he said.

I did, still rubbing my head.

The king of Sounis was not polished. Nor was he an impressive bearlike man the way kings were in my mother's fairy tales. He was too short and too oily, and he was a shade too fat to be elegant. But he was shrewd. He routinely doubled his taxes and kept a large army to prevent any rebellion by his citizens. The taxes supported the army, and when the army itself became a threat, he sent it off to fight with his neighbors. Their victories enriched the treasury. The kingdom of Sounis was bigger than it had been anytime since the invaders had broken off pieces of it to award to their allies. The king had driven the Attolians out of their land on the Sounis side of the Hephestial Mountains, forcing them back through the narrow pass through the country of Eddis to the Attolian homeland on the far side. There were rumors that he wanted to annex land there as well and that Attolia was preparing for all-out war.

Ignoring his magus, Sounis walked over to the bench on the wall beside my chair. He pulled a small casket off it and carried it to the magus's desk, where he tipped its contents out. A cascade of double-heavy gold coins. A single one would buy a family's farm and all its livestock. Several pieces fell and rang on the stone floor. One landed by my foot and lay staring up at me like a yellow eye.

I almost bent to pick it up but stopped myself and said instead, "My uncle used to keep that much under his bed and count it every night."

"Liar," said the king. "You've never seen that much gold before in your life."

He couldn't know that I'd overstayed my welcome one night while creeping through his megaron and had crawled up through the space where the pipes of the hypocaust ran to hide in his treasure room. I had slept for a day in stuffy darkness on the ridged tops of his treasure trunks.

Sounis tapped the chest, lying empty on its side in front of him. "This is the gold that I am going to offer as a reward if you fail to bring back what I am sending you for. I'll offer it to anyone, from this country or any other, who brings you to me." He tipped the casket upright and snapped the lid down.

I felt my stomach dropping. It would be hard to outrun a reward like that. I'd be hunted from one end of the world to the other.

"I'd want you alive of course," said the king, and carefully described the grisly things that would happen to me when I was captured. I tried to stop listening after the first few examples, but he went on and on, and I was mesmerized like a bird in front of a snake. The magus stood with his hands across his chest and listened just as carefully. He didn't seem nervous anymore. He must have been satisfied that the king had accepted his plans and that his threats would encourage me in my work. My stomach felt worse and worse.

My cell, when I was returned to it, felt warm and safe by comparison to the magus's study. As soon as the guards were gone, I lay down on my stone bench and dumped the king and his threats out of my head without ceremony. They were too unpleasant to worry over anyway. I concentrated on a vision of myself leaving the prison. I made myself as comfortable as possible and went to sleep.

chapter 2

TWO GUARDS CAME FOR ME late the next morning, and I was surprised again. I had thought that the traveling the magus had mentioned would take some time to plan for. He had clearly gotten the king's approval for the plan only the previous night. My hopes, which had been falling and rising, sank again as I realized that the magus hadn't mentioned how far we would travel. It might be no more than a few miles. But I cheered up once I was free of my chains.

The guards removed the manacles this time as well as the waist and ankle cuffs. There were no clanking noises to accompany us as we walked down the gallery past the row of cell doors to the guardroom. The only sound was the tramp of feet, the guards', not mine, and the creaking of the leather jackets that they wore under their steel breastplates. We crossed through the guardroom to the door to the courtyard between the prison and the megaron. When the door opened, I learned in an instant that the light of the lamps the night before had been nothing to compare with the sun itself.

It was nearly noon, and the sunlight dropped directly into the courtyard. The pale yellow of the stones in the walls reflected it from all sides. I howled and swore as I covered my head with my arms and hunched over in pain. Burning at the stake couldn't have been worse.

It's a funny thing that the new gods have been worshiped in Sounis since the invaders came, but when people need a truly satisfying curse, they call on the old gods. I called on all of them, one right after another, and used every curse I'd overheard in the lower city. "Gods damn, *gods* damn," I was howling as the guards led me, completely blind, down the stairs. I still had my hands over my eyes, and they held me firmly by the elbows. My feet hardly touched the stone steps.

At the bottom the magus was waiting. He told me to pull myself together.

"Gods damn you, too," I said through my hands. One of the guards gave me a brisk shake, and I almost cursed him as well but decided to concentrate on the pain in my eyes. It didn't fade much, but after a few minutes, when I tilted my hands a little away from my face and looked down, I could make out the flagstones through my tears. I sniffed a little and wiped the tears away. As soon as I could manage, I pulled my hands farther from my face and tried to see what was happening around me in the courtyard. I had plenty of time.

There was an incredible amount of noise as horses crashed back and forth across the flagstones and the magus shouted at people. Not far away someone was unpacking a brace of saddle-bags and scattering the contents under the feet of a nervous horse. The horse kept sidling away from the mess and was dragged back by the groom holding its head. Evidently something was missing from the saddlebags. With more swearing the magus sent the unpacker back into the castle to fetch whatever it was.

"Look for it on the bench next to the retort," shouted the magus at the disappearing figure. "That's where it was when I told you to pack it the first time. Idiot," he muttered under his breath.

By the time the idiot returned, I could see he was carrying a small square leather case, which he dropped into the saddlebag. He then shoveled the waiting piles back in on top of it. The noise in the courtyard diminished as the magus stopped shouting and the horses calmed down.

I was still looking at the world through tears and the narrowest of slits between my eyelids. I counted the hazy shapes in front of me. It didn't seem like a large party, only five horses, but all of them had humped baggage behind their saddles. It was going to be a long trip. I grinned with satisfaction. Beside me the magus looked up at the sky and said to no one in particular, "I had planned to leave at daybreak. Pol," he shouted, "get the boys mounted. I'll load the thief."

I didn't appreciate the way he spoke of me as another parcel to be dumped into a saddlebag or, in my case, a saddle. He walked over to a horse, and I could see that he gestured to me to join him, but I didn't move. I hate horses. I know people who think that they are noble, graceful animals, but regardless of what a horse looks like from a distance, never forget that it is as likely to step on your foot as look at you.

"What?" I dissembled.

"Get on the horse, you idiot."

"Me?"

"Of course you, you fool."

I didn't move, and the magus got tired of waiting. He stepped to my side, grabbed me by the back of the neck, and hauled me over to the horse. I set my heels in and resisted. If I was going to climb onto an animal eight times my size, I wanted to plan the attempt first.

The magus was a good bit stronger than I was. Holding me by the cloth at the back of my neck, he shook once or twice and my head swam. I heard the cheap cloth tear. He grabbed for a firmer grip on my neck.

"Put your left foot in the stirrup," he said. "Your left one."

I did as I was told, and two of the grooms stepped over to lever me into the saddle before my brains had settled. Once up, I shook the hair back out of my eyes. As I tried to get it to hook behind my ears, I looked around. Being six feet off the ground does give one a sense of superiority. I shrugged my shoulders and crossed my arms, but the animal underneath me lurched sideways, and I had to uncross them in order to snatch at the front of the saddle. I held on while I waited for the others to mount.

Once the others were up, the magus directed his mount toward the archway at one side of the courtyard. My horse obediently followed, and the others came behind me as we passed under rooms of the palace and hallways that I had been in the night before. My eyes had a few moments of relief before we reached the outer gate. There was no fanfare, no shouting crowds to wish us luck on our journey—just as well. The only time I had been the focus of shouting crowds had been my trial, and I hadn't enjoyed that at all.

We weren't leaving through the main gate of the megaron, so we emptied out into a narrow street, only a little wider than the horses. My feet brushed against the whitewashed walls on either side. We twisted through more narrow streets until we reached the Sacred Way, which we followed down to the gate out of the old city. The gate was made out of blocks of stone bigger across than I am tall. Something else supposedly built by the old gods, it was topped by a solid stone lintel with two carved lions that were supposed to roar if an enemy of the king passed beneath them. At least they were said to be lions. The stone had been weathered by the centuries, and only indistinct monster figures remained, facing each other over a short pillar. They remained silent as we passed under.

The King's Route was wide and straight, crossing the more circuitous Sacred Way twice again before reaching the docks. When first built, the route had been bordered by stone walls that defended this road that connected the city to its harbor and its ships. The Long Walls were later dismantled to provide building materials for each new wing of the king's megaron as it grew from a one-room stronghold to a four-story palace.

As we rode onto the avenue, the sound of our horses' hooves was muddled with the other noises of the city. It was just before midday, and we were in the middle of the last surge of activity before people withdrew into their homes to wait out the afternoon heat. There were a few other horses on the road, and many more donkeys. People traveled on foot and in sedan chairs carried by servants. Merchants brought their goods up the avenue in carts and then led loaded donkeys down the narrow alleys to the back doors of the great houses, hoping to sell their vegetables to the cook, their linen to the housekeeper, or their wine to the steward. There was jostling and shouting and noise, and I relished it after the perpetual smothered quiet of the prison.

We threaded our way through the traffic, drawing curious looks. My companions were dressed in sturdy traveling clothes. I was still in the clothes I had worn to prison. My tunic had started life a cheerful yellow that I'd thought was dashing when I'd gotten it from a merchant in the lower city. It had faded to a greasy beige color. In addition to the smaller tears in the elbows, it had a larger one across my shoulders, thanks to the ministrations of the king's magus. I wondered what he thought I was going to wear if he persisted in shredding my clothes.

We crossed the upper part of the Sacred Way, and then the lower part, which held all the nicest shops in the city. Looking up and down it from the intersection, I could see the sedan chairs and fancy carriages waiting by doorways while the gently bred owners made their purchases inside. One shop near the corner sold only earrings, and I watched wistfully as it went by. We were too far away and there was too much traffic to allow even a glimpse of the merchandise displayed in its window.

Once we got to the lower town, traffic thinned out as people retreated indoors. I looked in vain for a familiar face. I wanted to tell someone I knew that I was free, but I didn't know very many people who would be out on the street in the middle of the day. When we reached the docks, we turned and rode along beside them toward the north gate out of the city. We passed the merchant ships and a pier full of private boats for fishing and pleasure and then the king's warships lined up at their docks. I was counting the cannons bolted to their decks and almost didn't see Philonikes passing by me.

"Philonikes!" I yelled, leaning out of the saddle. "Hey, Philonikes!" It was as much as I said before the magus grabbed my arm and dragged me away. He kicked his horse into a trot, and mine as well, as he hauled me down the street. I turned backward to wave to Philonikes disappearing around a corner, but I am not sure that he recognized me. The magus turned another corner before we slowed down, the other four riders hurrying to catch up.

"Damn it!" said the magus. "What do you think you are doing?"

I pointed backward and looked bewildered. "Philo's a friend of mine. I was going to say hello."

"Do you think I want everyone in the city to know that you are out working for the king?"

"Why not?"

"Do you announce that you're going off to steal something before you start?" He thought for a second. "Yes, you do. Well, I don't."

"Why not?" I asked again.

"None of your business. Just keep your mouth shut, do you understand?"

"Sure." I shrugged.

The knot we made of horses and riders in the middle of the street broke up as we restarted our journey. I ducked my head to hide my smile as my horse clopped along after the magus's.

At the north gate we went once again through a cool tunnel, this one much longer than the one through the megaron. It passed under the sloping earthwork and newer city wall. Then we were out in the sunshine again. Not that the city ended at the walls. The invaders in their officious and sensible way had brought prosperity to the city, and it had never stopped growing larger than its boundaries. We rode past the fine houses of the merchants who chose not to live squeezed into the city. Over the tops of garden walls we could see the citrus, the fig, and the almond trees, shading the grass or the edge of a veranda. The horses provided a sort of moving platform, allowing glimpses into other people's privacy. I would have preferred to climb the walls and look my fill. I didn't like the way the view kept disappearing behind the dark green leaves of an orange tree just as I got interested.

Beyond the villas the farms began. The fields stretched perfectly flat on either side of us for miles in every direction. There was not even an undulation in the ground, it seemed, until the road reached the foothills of the Hephestial Mountains, many miles ahead of us. Somewhere on our right, between us and the sea, should have been the river Seperchia, but I couldn't see it, even from the back of a horse. I stood up in my stirrups to look, but I could only guess that the water was hidden behind a line of trees that grew along its banks. My knees began to quiver after only a moment, so I sat down again. The horse made a little huffing noise of complaint.

"Don't pull on the reins," the man on my right said.

I looked down at the pieces of leather held in my hands and dropped them altogether. The animal obviously knew where it was going without my guidance. We passed field after field of onions and an occasional smaller field of cucumber or watermelon. The watermelons were as big as my head, so it was later in the summer than I'd thought. It had taken a long time to get out of prison.

We rode on through the heat. The late-summer winds, the etesians, hadn't come yet, and nothing moved in the entire landscape. The sun beat down, and even the dust didn't try to rise. We passed a grove of olive trees set out in front of a farmhouse. Their silver green leaves could have been carved out of stone.

In the city I had wanted to hug the sunlight and wrap it around myself like a blanket. I'd turned my body in the saddle in order to expose as much of my skin as possible to direct light. It was pleasant at first, but by the time the city was a single lump of gold stone behind us, I felt as if I were wearing a coat of dirt and dried sweat that had shrunk to be two sizes too small. I itched everywhere. The smells of the prison floated down the road with me, and I think that even the horse underneath me objected.

I noticed that as the sun got hotter, the two riders on either side of me moved farther and farther away.

I looked over the party. The magus I had already studied. On my right was the soldier who warned me about pulling on the reins. His profession was obvious, as was the sword tucked under the flap of one of his saddlebags I guessed that he was the Pol that the magus had shouted to in the courtyard, because the other two members of the group were certainly the boys. One younger and one several years older, I guessed, than myself. Why they were with us, I couldn't imagine. The older one also had a sword in a scabbard, and with coaching he could probably chop up a straw man, but the younger one looked to be completely useless. They were both obviously well bred, not servants, and I wondered if they were brothers. Like the magus, they were dressed in dark blue tunics that flared at the waist over their trousers. The older one had darker hair and was the better-looking. He looked as if he knew it. Riding on my left, he wrinkled his nose whenever a small wind wafted from my direction, but he never looked over at me. The younger boy rode mostly behind me, and every time I turned my head to glance at him, I found him staring back. I identified them as Useless the Elder and Useless the Younger for the time being.

The heat grew intolerable, and I grew more exhausted with every lurch of the horse I was riding. After what seemed like hours of swaying in the saddle, I realized that a fall was inevitable if we didn't stop. "I'm tired," I said. "I'm tired."

There was no response; the magus didn't even turn his head, so I made a decision for myself. I slid sideways down one side of the horse, trusting that the leg I left behind would come after me. It did, though not gracefully; the horse was still moving as I reached the ground, and I had to hop a few steps on one leg until my other leg caught up. Once I had both feet planted in the dust of the road, I headed for the grass beside it. I stepped into a ditch and, coming out of it, stumbled onto my knees and then onto my stomach and didn't get up.

The soldier must have come after me like a shot. I felt his

fingers grab for my shirt as I fell. Everyone else dismounted and trooped across the ditch as well, until they were standing around me in a half circle. I opened my eyes for a moment to look at their boots, then closed them again.

"What's the matter with him, magus?" It must have been the younger one that asked.

"Gods damn. We're only halfway to Methana, and I wanted to get to Matinaea tonight. He's exhausted, that's all. Not enough food to keep him going. No, just leave him," as someone prodded me with a boot.

Oh, thank gods, I thought. They're going to leave me. All I wanted to do was lie in the dry prickly grass with my feet in a ditch forever. I could be a convenient sort of milemarker, I thought. Get to the thief and you know you are halfway to Methana. Wherever Methana might be.

But they didn't leave me. They unsaddled their horses and got out their lunches and sat and ate while I slept.

When the sun was halfway down the sky, Pol nudged me with one foot until I woke up. I twitched my eyes open and had no idea at all where I was. I wasn't in bed. I wasn't at home. I'd woken up several times disoriented in the prison, and I automatically stifled my first thrash of surprise to prevent my chains from grinding on old bruises, and finally I remembered that there were no chains. I crossed one arm over my face and moaned convincingly. I felt surprisingly well. I was as hungry as a donkey, but my head was clear. I sat up and rubbed at the stiffness on the side of my face where the grass had left its rough pattern.

I groaned and complained while Pol, single-handed, pushed me back up onto the horse and we all started down the road again. The magus rode beside me and handed me pieces of cheese and lumps of bread that he tore off a loaf as we went. I ate with one hand and held on with the other. Horses are the most awful means of transport. I wanted to ask why they hadn't brought a cart, but I was too busy eating.

We made it to Methana as the sun was going down. It was a small town with just a few houses and an inn at an intersection of roads. We didn't stop. We rode on until it was pitch-dark. The moon was just a tiny sickle, and the soldier dismounted to lead his horse. He walked slowly to avoid stepping into the ditch by the roadside, and the other horses followed his.

The night air was cool, but my wonderful nap was a long way behind me. I balanced on the narrow back of my horse and wished the saddle offered more support. My head drooped forward and then bobbed back. The magus must have had eyes like a thief because he told Pol to stop and dismounted to walk alongside me, one hand resting just above my knee, ready to shake me if I fell asleep. He shook hard and resorted to pinching periodically.

We reached Matinaea at last. It was no bigger than Methana had been, but more roads met there. The inn was two stories tall and had a gate beside it that led to an enclosed courtyard. As we rode up, a groomsman came to take the horses. We all slid to the ground, and Pol was quickly beside me with one hand firmly on my shoulder. It was an easy business for him; my shoulder came only to his chest. Sometimes it bothers me that I am so small. It bothered me then, and I shrugged my shoulder in irritation, but his hand didn't move.

The magus introduced himself as a traveling landholder to the owner of the inn and said that he had sent a messenger ahead to arrange rooms. The owner was delighted to see him, and we all trooped toward the doorway. As I passed the owner's wife, her nose wrinkled, and as I reached the door, she protested.

"That one," she accused, pointing at me. "It's that one that smells so awful, and he's not coming into my wineroom and I won't have him sleeping in any of my clean beds."

Her husband made futile hushing motions with his hands.

"No, I won't have it. Not if he's your lordship's son," she said to the magus. "Although I hope he's not."

I could feel my face getting hot as the blood rushed all the way up to my ears. The magus and the woman negotiated, over the husband's protests. The magus said no, I couldn't sleep in the barn, but I could sleep on the floor. He gave her an extra silver coin and promised I would wash immediately. She gave directions to the pump in the courtyard, and Pol led me away.

The pump was in the middle of the courtyard behind the inn. There were stables on two sides, a wall on the third and the back of the inn completed the courtyard. It was not a private place to take a bath. When we reached the pump, Pol grabbed my shirt at the waist and jerked it upward. I snapped my arms down to prevent it from going over my head. The fabric tore in his hands. He reached for me again, but I stepped away, drowsiness gone.

"This," I snapped, "I can do for myself."

"Just make sure it's a good job," he said before he began to pump. The water gushed out of a pipe at the height of my waist as I stripped out of my overshirt and dumped it on the cobbles. I pulled off my shoes. I had no stockings, so the pants followed immediately after. As the water splashed off the cobblestones and onto my naked legs, gooseflesh came out under the dirt. I shivered and swore as I bent into the stream.

While I rinsed under the pump, the younger Useless arrived. He kept well away from the splattering water.

"Put those down in a dry spot," said Pol, "and fetch a couple of sacks from the stable."

When Useless came back, Pol took one of the sacks he'd

brought and handed it to me with a square block of soap. Crouching beside the water, I soaked the sack and rubbed the soap across it. It made a tremendous lather, and I stopped to smell it in surprise. I laughed. It was the magus's scented soap. Useless the Younger must have dug it out of one of the saddlebags.

I scrubbed myself with the sacking, washing away what felt like years of dirt. I rubbed hard and then rinsed and soaped myself up again before Pol could stop pumping water. I dragged the sack across the back of my neck and as much of my shoulders as I could reach and scrubbed my face again and again, thinking to myself that my nose would be smaller, but at least it would be clean.

The younger Useless stood and watched, and I wondered what he thought of me. The iron waistband had left deep bruises in a circle around my waist, and I was covered in flea bites and sores, but the ones on my wrists were the worst. Where the manacles had chafed there were raw spots partially covered in scabs that were black against my prison-fair skin. Once I had cleaned most of the dirt off myself and rinsed my hair, I squatted down in front of the spraying water and tried to find the place where the water would fall most gently on my wrists. Several of the sores were infected, and they needed to be cleaned out, but it was going to be a painful business. My whole body was shaking with the cold, and I clenched my teeth to keep them from chattering while I leaned into the water.

Pol stepped around the pump and leaned over me to look at the sores. The water flow slackened.

"Leave them," he said. "I'll work on them inside." He gave me another piece of sacking to dry off with, and when I was done, he handed me a pile of clothes—pants and a shirt as well as an overshirt and a pair of stout workboots. I looked around for my own clothes and saw the younger Useless disappearing into the stable with them in his arms.

"Hey," I yelled. "Come back with those!"

He turned around uncertainly. "Magus told me to burn them," he said.

"Everything but my shoes!"

Useless looked into the pile in his arms and wrinkled his nose. "All right, but if Magus says to burn them, you'll have to give them back."

"Fine, fine," I said as I hopped across the wet cobblestones in my bare feet and took my shoes out of his arms. The rest of the clothing I consigned to the fires without regret, but I'd had the shoes made specially. They were low boots just a little higher than my ankles, reinforced on the soles, but still supple enough to let me move unsuspected through other people's houses. I carried them back to Pol; then I looked for a dry place to stand while I got dressed. The pants were heavy cotton and bagged at the ankle where they tucked into my shoes. They bagged even more around my waist, but there was a belt to hold them up. The shirt was cotton as well. There was something wonderful about rubbing a clean shirt against clean skin. I was smiling by the time I pulled the overshirt over my head. It was dark blue and short-sleeved. It came down to my thighs and was enough too big that when I moved my arms across my chest, it didn't bind. I checked to be sure.

"Gods bless that magus, he thinks of everything, doesn't he?" I said to Pol. He grunted and waved me toward the inn's back door.

We went inside to the taproom, where the magus and the two Uselesses were waiting for us. There were deep bowls of stew set out on the table, but before Pol would let me have mine, he wanted to look at my wrists. The magus looked over his shoulder and then sent the elder Useless up to his room to get a relief kit with bandages and little pots of salve in it.

Pol got one of the lanterns off the wall and put it on the table beside him. The landlady tsk-tsked and brought out a bowl of warm water, a cloth, and more soap. Pol started to work on the right wrist first, while I looked at my dinner regretfully. After he had rinsed it with the soapy water, he rubbed a little salve on top of the scabs on the two sores, one above each of the bones in my wrist. Then he wrapped the wrist carefully in a clean white bandage. It was a tidy job, and I was impressed. I was off my guard when he took up my left arm. There was just one sore, but it ran all the way across the top of my wrist. Instead of a scab it had raw patches and bubbles of fluid trapped under flaps in the skin. Without any warning, Pol slid a knife under one of the flaps and twisted it open.

I screamed at the top of my lungs. Everyone in the room jumped, including Pol, but his knife was well away from my wrist by then. I struggled to get out of his grip, but he had his hand clamped on my forearm, and he held on like a vise. I tried with my right hand to pry his fingers loose, but they didn't budge. As I went on yelling and twisting his fingers, Pol without a word put his knife down on the table and reached into the relief kit. What he brought out was the wooden gag they put in someone's mouth before doing something drastic like cutting off a leg. He held it up in front of my face.

"That's enough," he said.

I thought about explaining that that sore had been there for weeks. I'd been so careful not to let the manacles bang it, and I'd favored it and done everything I could to keep it from hurting anymore and he could have warned me before he stuck his great godsdamned knife into it. But I looked at the gag in his hand and shut my mouth. I contented myself with wiggling and whimpering a little as he opened each of the infected spots, cleaned the entire sore, and rubbed salve onto it. When he had it wrapped in a bandage, I sniffed and wiped my nose and turned to the table to eat my dinner.

Useless the Elder was looking at me in amusement. "Not exactly stalwart, are you?" he said.

I told him what he could do with his own dinner and got a poke in the rib cage from Pol's elbow. I sulked through the first few bites of my stew before I noticed how good it was. While I savored it, I listened to the others talking and gathered that the older Useless was named Ambiades and the younger Sophos. They weren't related to each other, but they were both apprentices of the magus. I ate until I was too exhausted to keep my head up anymore and fell asleep on the table with the last bite still in my mouth.

chapter 3

_I_ WOKE IN THE MORNING in one of the inn's upstairs rooms, lying on the floor. From where I lay, I could see the webbing underneath the bed next to me and how much it sagged under Pol's weight. He must have carried me in and laid me out on the rug before going to sleep himself. I looked enviously at his bed, but at least I was on a wood floor, not a stone one. There was a rug underneath me and a blanket pulled over me.

I reached up with one hand and pushed the hair off my face. I usually wore it long enough to wrap into a stubby braid at the base of my neck, but it had grown beyond that in prison. Sometime during my arrest I had lost the tie that held it, and it had been hanging down in my face and tangling into knots ever since. The previous night's rinsing had washed out some of the dirt, but the tangles were still there. I thought about borrowing a knife from Pol and cutting it all off but discarded the idea. Pol wouldn't lend me the knife, but he'd cut the hair off himself, and that would be painful. Besides, I liked my hair long. When it was clean and pulled back from my face, I liked to think it gave me an aristocratic look, and it was useful. I sometimes caught small items in the hair at the top of the braid and hid them there.

Still, matted and tangled, the hair was not aristocratic. I pushed it off my forehead for the time being and sat up. Pol's eyes opened as I moved, and I discarded any thoughts of sneaking away even before I discovered that I was chained to the bed. My ankle was padded by someone's spare shirt, and locked around it was an iron cuff with a chain that looped around the leg of the bed. Only by lifting the bed, with Pol in it, could I have gotten free. I wondered whose idea the shirt and the blanket had been. Pol didn't seem like a man sensitive to personal comforts.

I had another wash, this time with warm water in a washroom at the end of the hallway outside the room. The magus and his two apprentices were already there, stripped to the waist, splashing water around as they got themselves clean. They looked up as Pol and I came in, and I could see that they all three expected me to resent more soap and water.

"I washed last night," I pointed out to the magus. "Look"— I held up my arms—"I'm very clean. Why am I washing again?"

The magus stepped away from the basin that held his shaving water and caught one of my arms. He was careful to grip it above the clean white bandages before he turned my hand over and held it up to my face so that I could see the black dirt still ingrained in the folds of my skin.

"Wash," he commanded, and before I could protest further, Pol grabbed me from behind and pushed me over toward an empty basin lying next to the others on a shelf that ran waist height along the wall. Holding the back of my neck with one hand, he lifted a pitcher with another and poured steaming water into the basin.

"I can wash myself," I pointed out to no effect.

He added a washing cloth and soap and went to work on my face. When I opened my mouth to complain, I got soap in it. I attempted to slip away, but could not. The hand Pol had on my neck stretched easily from one side of it to the other. He was merciless to my bruises, and I did my best to stamp on his toes in retaliation. He squeezed harder on my neck until I stopped. He soaped my shoulders and bent me at the waist with another squeeze, in order to soap my back. Bent over, I saw that his knees were within reach. I might have grabbed one and thrown him to the floor, but I didn't try. This was no time to demonstrate unsuspected abilities. Besides, if I missed the grab, I would only look silly and I had had enough of that.

Pol rinsed off the soap with a pitcher of water. I pulled myself upright and tried to look disdainful, but the bath wasn't over. Pol marched me across the room to a wooden tub full of water and pushed my head under while I was still howling in outrage. He lifted me out, and while I coughed, he rubbed more soap into my hair and pushed me under again.

When the grip in his fingers finally lessened, I dragged myself away and threw myself, dripping water, to the other side of the bathroom. I watched him warily while I coughed the water out of my lungs. He stood patiently while I twisted water out of my hair. When I snarled that I could have more easily washed myself, he tossed me a towel, and then he lifted one arm and gestured leisurely with a finger toward the door.

His face was almost expressionless, but the corners of his mouth twitched. Jutting out my jaw to conceal the expression on my own face, I stalked down the hall and recovered my shirt and overshirt from the room where I had slept.

"You got my pants wet," I complained as I pulled on my shirt. The waistband was soaked.

Pol didn't respond.

I was still pulling my overshirt over my head as I thumped down the stairs to the taproom, where breakfast and the others were waiting. The magus and his apprentices were smiling at their food. I threw myself onto the end of the bench and ignored them.

After I had eaten one bowl of oatmeal, I combed my fingers through my hair to get it into some sort of order. Tearing a few knots apart in the process, I divided it into three clumps and wound the clumps over one another to make a short braid. Holding the end of the braid in one hand, I looked around the taproom for inspiration. Over my shoulder I saw a young woman at the bar. I smiled at her and circled one finger around the tip of the braid to show what I needed. When she smiled at me and waved one hand to show that she understood, I turned back to the table to meet the ferocious glare of Useless the Elder, whose name I remembered was Ambiades. I didn't know what had irritated him, so I directed my puzzled look on my oatmeal bowl.

A few minutes later the girl from the bar arrived with more breakfast for everyone and a piece of twine to tie off my hair. As she went away, she looked over at Useless the Elder and sniffed in contempt, so I had an explanation for the ferocious glare. No friend had I made there, but I wasn't with this group to make friends, and besides, he sneered too much. I've found that people who sneer are almost always sneering at me.

The magus, Pol, and the younger Useless, Sophos, were studiously eating their breakfasts.

"She seems like a nice girl," I said, and got an angry look from Ambiades and his master. The magus couldn't have been rebuffed by the barkeep, so I assumed that he didn't want me baiting his apprentice.

"Very friendly," I added for good measure before I dug into my second large bowl of oatmeal. It was a little bit gloppy, but there was butter and honey on top. There was a bowl of yogurt nearby, and I ate that as well. Sophos had a smaller bowl, and when the magus wasn't looking, I slipped it out from under his lifted spoon and switched it for my empty one. He looked startled, and Ambiades stifled a derisive laugh, but neither of them complained to the magus. There was another large bowl that held oranges in the middle of the table, and I was reaching for those when I noticed the magus's glare.

"I'm hungry," I said defensively, and took three. Two went into the pockets of the overshirt, and the third I peeled and was eating when the landlady arrived.

She came to ask us if we wanted a lunch packed, but she stopped in surprise when she saw me.

I gave her my best boyish grin. "I clean up nicely, don't I?" I said.

She smiled back. "Yes, you do. Where did you get so dirty?"

"Prison," I said.

"Ah," she said. People went to prison all the time. "I expect you're glad to get out."

"Yes, ma'am, especially because the food is so good."

She laughed and turned back to the magus, who was looking grim. "Was there anything else that you needed, sir?"

"No, we'll stop in Evisa for lunch, thank you."

Everyone went to pack up the horses except the magus and me. The two of us remained at the table until Pol sent Sophos in to tell us that everything was ready. There was a mounting block in the courtyard, so I was able to get onto my horse myself, although Pol held its head and Sophos held the stirrup for me and offered advice.

"You don't have to slither on that way," he said. "She isn't going to move out from underneath you."

"She might," I replied sourly.

As we rode our horses out of the courtyard, the landlady stepped out of the inn's front door with a napkin-wrapped bundle in her hand. She reached up to stop my horse with one hand, which was pretty fearless of her, but she seemed to think it was nothing out of the ordinary.

"A little something to eat while you're riding. It's a long way to Evisa." She handed the bundle up to me and added as she did so, "My youngest is down in the prison."

"Oh," I said, not surprised. They probably hadn't bribed the tax collector enough. "Don't worry too much," I said as the magus dragged my horse away. "It's not so bad." I forgot myself enough to give her a real smile but replaced it with a grin when I saw her face brighten in response.

"What a lie that was," I added under my breath as we left the inn behind. The road curved away between rows of olive trees. As soon as we were well out of sight, the magus pulled up his horse and mine as well.

He leaned across his saddle and smacked me on the head, then pulled away the bundle of lunch, which I had hung on a convenient buckle of the saddle.

"Hey!" I yelled in outrage. "That was for me!"

"I don't need you chatting up every barkeep between here and the mountains."

"I didn't say a word to the barkeep," I pointed out in an aggrieved tone as I rubbed the spot on my head where his heavy seal ring had hit. "Not a word. And I was only being polite to the landlady."

The magus lifted his hand to hit me again, but I leaned out of reach. "You can keep your civility," he snapped, "to yourself. You don't talk to anyone, do you understand?"

"So, so, so. Do I get my lunch back?"

No, I didn't Magus said we would have it later. I sulked for the next hour. I looked at my saddle and ignored the passing scenery—I'd seen onions before—until we rode by a field being harvested. The sweet, tangy smell woke my stomach. I sat up straight and looked around. "Hey," I called to the magus, "I'm hungry."

He ignored me, but I decided against prolonged sulking. It wasn't going to get me an early lunch, and my neck was sore, from bending over the saddle. I dug one of the oranges out of my pocket and began to peel it, dropping the rinds on the road. Outside the city I had felt like a bug caught out in the center of a tablecloth. Now the world was closing back in in a comforting way. The road rose slowly and dropped into an occasional hollow as we climbed the hills that led up to the mountains in the north of the country. The fields were smaller, and they were surrounded by olive trees, which grew where other crops wouldn't. Individual orchards were blending together into an undifferentiated forest of silver and gray. I wondered how the owners knew when their land stopped and someone else's began.

On my left Sophos asked, "Was it really not so bad?"

"Was what?"

"Prison."

I remembered my comment to the landlady. I watched Sophos for a minute, riding comfortably on the back of his well-bred mare.

"That prison," I said with heartfelt sincerity, "was absolutely the most awful thing that has happened to me in my entire life."

I could tell by the way he looked at me that he thought my life must have been filled with one awful thing after another.

"Oh," he said, and pressed his horse a little faster, in order to widen the space between us.

Pol continued to ride behind me. I looked over my shoulder at him and got a stony glare. I ate my orange and listened to the conversation between the magus, Sophos, and Ambiades. He was asking them questions. He wanted Sophos to tell him the classification of a eucalyptus tree. Sophos went on about this and that and whether it was fruit-bearing. Most of what he said I couldn't hear, but he seemed to have gotten it right because the magus told him he was pleased. Ambiades had more trouble with the olive tree, and the magus was not pleased. Ambiades shifted his horse a little farther away from the magus, and I gathered that cuffs to the head with that seal ring were not uncommon. The magus asked Sophos for the correct answer, and Sophos gave it, obviously embarrassed for Ambiades's sake.

"Sophos seems to have been paying attention, Ambiades. Would you like to hazard a guess why this sort of classification is important?"

"Not really," said Ambiades.

"Do it anyway," said the magus.

"Oh, I guess it's so you can tell which trees should be planted where."

"Go on."

But Ambiades couldn't think of anything else.

Sophos tried to help him out. "If you found a new tree, you might be able to tell if you could eat the fruit if you knew it was just like an olive tree?"

"If it was *just* like an olive tree it would *be* one," snapped Ambiades. I put all my weight onto one stirrup and leaned over. I wanted to get a look at Sophos's face to see if he was blushing. He was.

"Of course," the magus pointed out, "if you can't classify an olive, Ambiades, you wouldn't know one if you saw one, would you?"

I leaned over on the other stirrup. Now Ambiades was blushing. He was scowling as well.

"Try again with the fig tree," said the magus.

Ambiades poked and guessed his way through that classification, and I lost interest. I was getting tired. I ate my second orange.

Long before we reached Evisa, I was exhausted. I complained constantly that I was tired, but no one seemed to notice. I was also hungry. I told the magus I would starve in the saddle if I didn't get something to eat, and he finally, reluctantly, opened the bundle with my lunch in it. But he insisted on dividing it equally among Ambiades, Sophos, and myself, even though I pointed out that they couldn't possibly be as hungry as I was.

Ambiades nobly handed over some of his portion to me, but there was something about the way he did it that made my hackles rise.

It was late in the afternoon when we reached Evisa. The magus was disgruntled that we hadn't made better time. He hadn't reckoned on my outstanding skill with horses.

There was no inn at Evisa, but there was a woman who served food to travelers at a collection of tables under the trees in the town square. Ambiades and Sophos were equally horrified at the lunch—wrinkled olives and hard cheese—but the bread was soft and good. The yogurt had enough garlic in it to kill every vampire in the country. I ended up eating almost everything. It was hard to be a picky eater in the lower city of Sounis and impossible in the king's prison.

"I told you that they weren't hungry," I said to the magus. "I don't know why you didn't let me have all the meat pies." As I spoke, he pulled the bowl filled with shriveled olives out of my hand.

"You'll make yourself sick," he said.

I snagged a few more from the bowl as it was carried away, but I let the rest go. He was right. If I tried to force much more into my stomach, it was going to revolt. I tottered away from the table to a patch of grass, where I lay down and went to sleep. It seemed like only a few minutes before Pol was nudging me in the ribs again with his foot.

"Get up."

"Go away."

"I'll get you up," he warned.

"I don't want to get up. I want you to go away."

After he'd made sure that I was thoroughly awake, I told him that I hoped he was bitten by something poisonous in the next bed he slept in. I dragged myself up on one of the tables and looked at Ambiades, who was standing with the horses. "Bring mine over here," I said. "I'm not moving the table over there."

But Ambiades was not going to move a step at the request of a worthless and insolent petty criminal. Ambiades, I realized, was the kind of person who liked to put people in a hierarchy, and he wanted me to understand that I was at the bottom of his. He was supposed to treat me politely in spite of my subservient position, and I was supposed to be grateful.

For my part, I wanted Ambiades to understand that I considered myself a hierarchy of one. I might bow to the superior force of the magus and Pol, but I wasn't going to bow to him. Neither of us moved.

Pol and the magus went on studiously looking at the horse's legs, leaving Ambiades and me to sort ourselves out. Ambiades had gotten himself into an intractable difficulty whether he knew it or not. He was bigger than I was, certainly, but he had to assume I would put up a vicious and potentially embarrassing fight if he tried to force me over to the horse. Sophos saved him, taking the horse's reins and walking it over to the table.

Ambiades looked on in contempt, unaware, it seemed, that it was his dignity that Sophos had spared.

"Why didn't you bring a cart?" I grumbled to the magus as we rode out of the town.

"A what?"

"A cart—you know, a large wooden box on wheels, pulled by horses."

"Why would I have done that?" the magus asked, amused.

"So that I could be sleeping in the back of it right now."

"I didn't plan this trip with your comfort in mind," he said sourly.

"Damn right."

The horses ambled up the hills for another hour. The sun was setting when the magus finally grew disgusted and asked me if I thought I could stay on the horse's back if it trotted.

"Probably not," I told him honestly. By that time I was too tired to be optimistic.

"You'll have to learn sooner or later. We're not walking all the way. Ambiades," he shouted, "ride back here and show him how to trot." So Ambiades, who had gotten several hundred yards ahead of us, turned around and trotted his horse back.

"Nice seat." Pol was just behind me, and I was a little surprised that he spoke without being spoken to first. The magus passed the compliment along to Ambiades, but he only scowled. He seemed as disgruntled by praise as he was by badgering.

"Now you, Sophos," the magus called, and Sophos obeyed. Even I could see that he didn't ride as well as Ambiades. I looked back at Pol to see what his opinion was. He winced.

The magus commiserated, "Too bad you can't take Ambiades home to be duke and let me keep Sophos to be magus."

"He's going to be a duke?" I said, surprised. One didn't usually find a future duke as an apprentice of anyone. I didn't expect an answer, but Ambiades supplied one of a sort.

"If his father doesn't strangle him first," he said.

My lesson in horseback riding became a lesson for Sophos as well. The three of us fell back while Ambiades and the magus trotted ahead.

"Pol thinks you ride like a sack of loose rocks," Ambiades told Sophos before he left. Sophos reddened, and Pol told Ambiades to get moving. A little later we heard pieces of a lecture the magus was giving him about plant classification and its importance. I tried to pay attention to both the lecture and the riding instructions but eventually gave up and listened to Pol.

He was explaining that the horse's shoulder lifted not when the foot did but when the foot came down. "Now," said Pol, "hold up your hand like this." He held it up as if he were blessing the fields beside him. Sophos imitated him, and Pol smacked him hard in the palm with his fist. When Pol told him to hold the hand back up, he did, but he jerked it backward and Pol's second blow barely touched him. It was a simple lesson that my father had taught me years ago. If you think you are going to be hit, at least try to move out of the way. My father taught it to me with the flat side of his sword.

Pol explained to Sophos, and incidentally to me, that if you are already rising when the horse's shoulder bumps your backside, you have a more comfortable ride. So we tried trotting up the road, lifting our backsides just ahead of our horses' rising shoulders and moving a little faster toward wherever we were going. Very soon I didn't have the strength to lift myself out of the saddle, and my brains bounced in my head the rest of the day.

We walked the horses frequently to rest them and me, but I

was nearly dead by nightfall, and I didn't see much of the town where we stopped. It had an inn. We went in and I ate, and before I was full, I fell asleep on the table.

I woke up on the floor again, next to Pol's bed, but this time Ambiades and Sophos were in the room as well, sharing the bed on the other side of me. I contemplated the undignified sort of figure I must have made as I was carried upstairs a second time and winced.

Pol was awake with the first clink of my chain, and I wondered if I could have slept the entire night without shifting. I may have. Or he'd woken often to check on me. When he saw that I was awake, he swung his feet out of the bed and nudged me aside in order to make room for them on the floor.

"Rouse yourselves," he grunted to the two in the other bed.

Ambiades untangled himself from the sheets and crawled out of the bed. Yawning, he padded over to the chair where everyone else's clothes were piled. I'd slept in mine. Sophos didn't move. I sat up and looked over the edge of the bed. His eyelids could have been glued shut.

"Psst!" Ambiades hissed, but it was too late. Pol reached over me and woke Sophos as efficiently as he had woken me after lunch the day before, but at least Sophos landed on a soft bed. Once everyone was up, we all headed outdoors for the bench-house and a bath at the pump. The sun was just rising over the hills, the sky was blue and clear, but the hollow in which the town sat was still dark. The water was cold, but I was the only one that complained. I warned Pol that if he tried to wash me again, I'd bite.

"He's probably septic," Ambiades warned, teasing me in a tone just a little more condescending than the one he used on Sophos.

Pol handed me a washcloth without a word and watched while I scrubbed the last of the prison dirt off my elbows and ankles and the back of my neck. The magus's soap smelled of honey-suckle.

Inside the inn our breakfast waited: oatmeal and yogurt. There were no oranges this time. "What was the thumping this morning?" the magus asked Pol as we sat down. He was looking at me.

"That one," the soldier answered, pointing at Sophos with his spoon, "would sleep through cannon fire. One morning he won't wake up until someone spits him on a longspear."

Sophos blushed.

"Sleeping lightly is a necessary virtue in a soldier," the magus pointed out to him, "and it's not a fault in anyone else."

"So who wants to be a soldier?" Sophos grumbled at his oatmeal.

"Not me," I said. Everyone else at the table looked at me in surprise, as if they had forgotten I could talk.

"Who asked you?" Ambiades sneered.

"He did, fuzz-lip." I pointed with my spoon to Sophos while Ambiades's hand leapt to his face.

He jerked it back down and asked, "What would scum from a gutter know about being a soldier?"

"I wouldn't know, not being scum from a gutter. But my father is a soldier, and it's a bloody, thankless, useless job for people who are too stupid and too ugly to do anything else." Even if my father and I have come to appreciate each other a little more, I still don't think much of his chosen profession, but I probably shouldn't have mentioned it then. My capacity for tact sometimes surprises even myself.

There was a perfect silence at the table while all of us looked over at Pol to see what he would make of this insult to his intelligence as well as his manners. He remained impassive, but the magus told me that in the future I could ignore conversation that was not directed toward me and I should keep my mouth closed unless specifically addressed. I remembered that I had been brought along as a useful sort of tool and not a human being at all.

I ate my breakfast in silence. When the magus stood up and said, "We'd better get the horses ready," I continued to stare at my empty oatmeal bowl until he cuffed me on the back of the head.

"What?" I said. "Were you specifically addressing me? I thought I was supposed to ignore those—"

"I have a riding crop packed in my saddlebags," he said. "Would you like me to use it on you?" He was bending over me, and his voice was low. I am not sure that anyone else heard, but I understood him plainly. I threw one leg over the bench and stood up.

"Lead on," I said.

Several extra packages were added to our baggage before we rode away from the inn. While Ambiades, Sophos, and I watched, Pol and the magus carefully arranged and rearranged the loads so that the horses would not be unevenly weighted. I wondered about Pol. He wasn't a common foot soldier. Sophos and even Ambiades treated him with too much deference. The magus clearly liked and respected him, relying on him to enforce orders addressed to me. He'd probably be the one to use the riding crop if push came to shove.

As we left the town, it became clear why the magus hadn't brought a cart. There was no road for it to travel on beyond this small nameless town, or nothing that a civilized person, used to the streets of a city, would call a road. The wagon track we'd been following since Evisa had been carefully maintained, its central grassy strip and its verges kept cropped by the goats of each small village we passed through. That route divided, turning west to head along the foothills, or east to intersect the main road that led to the pass through the Hephestial Mountains. We headed straight on the track that showed fewer signs of travel.

We passed a few more farms, and then the way narrowed even further to a skinny, overgrown path with high grass and scrubby oaks growing on either side, sometimes so close that pricking leaves caught at the fabric in my trousers.

The path climbed steeply in places. The horses worked hard. In single file they heaved themselves uphill with a constant clatter of small stones. I gripped the horse underneath as firmly as I could with my knees and worried about slipping off the back end of the saddle at every rise in the trail. I held on with both hands as well, but my arms were in no better shape than my legs, and by midmorning they shook with the strain.

"Hey, why don't we stop for lunch?"

The magus looked at me in disgust, but when we reached the next open space, he directed his horse onto the grass, and mine obediently followed. I tried to convince it to move into the shade before I climbed down, but it stopped next to the magus's horse and wouldn't go on.

"Why doesn't this damned horse go where I want it to?" I asked, exasperated.

"Stop jerking on the reins like that. It won't move," the magus told me.

"So I've found," I said as I slid down. "It must like your horse more than I like you."

Sophos heard me and laughed. "It's a packhorse," he explained. "It's trained to stop next to its leader."

"Really?" I looked at the horse beside me in surprise. "Are they that smart?"

"Smarter than you," said Ambiades, coming up beside us.

"I never heard of a horse that could steal a king's seal," I pointed out with a smirk of my own.

"That's what I meant," said Ambiades.

"Why don't you eat hot coals?" I walked over to where Pol was taking food out of the bag. I noticed Sophos staring after me.

"What?" I snapped at him, and he looked away.

Ambiades put the words in his mouth. "He wants to know if you really are stupid enough to bet a man that you could steal the king's seal and then show it as proof the next day in a wineshop."

It had been a professional risk, but there was no point in saying so. I turned my back on them both.

We had more bread and olives and cheese for lunch. When I wanted more, the magus said no. "I can't be sure that we will have more provisions until we get through the mountains."

I looked at the packages still tied to the horses. "You didn't bring enough."

"We should pick up a little more tonight. You won't starve."

"No, that's true," I said. "You can always give me some of Ambiades's food."

The magus gave me an ugly look. "You'll get your share and nothing else. No one's going hungry so that *you* can eat."

"I don't see why not," I said as I lay down in the grass for a nap. It had dried in the summer sun to crackling stalks that poked me in the arms and neck. "I'm a lot more important than anyone else here," I told the blue sky above me.

No one replied, and after a few minutes I fell asleep.

chapter 4

*W*E STOPPED AGAIN early in the evening. Earlier than the magus wanted. He grumbled but agreed to look for a campsite after watching me nearly slide over the back end of my horse at one steep spot in the trail. As soon as he chose a place to stop, I dismounted and collapsed in the prickly grass. I lay there while the magus directed the unpacking of the horses and listened as Ambiades carefully and condescendingly instructed Sophos in the construction of a cooking fire. I turned my head to watch.

"Haven't you ever stayed out overnight hunting?" Ambiades asked, looking at kindling tightly stacked in a poor imitation of a campfire.

Sophos cast an embarrassed look at Pol. "Not alone," he said.

"Well, Your Highness," Ambiades teased, "if you stack all the wood one piece directly on top of another, it won't burn. The fire suffocates. Imagine how you would feel if you had all that wood stacked on top of you. Watch." He dismantled the pile and built a pointed hut of sticks with the skill of much practice. "Make a house and the fire lives in it; make a gravepile and the fire dies. Understand?"

"Yes," said Sophos humbly, and stepped aside to allow Pol space to cook. I didn't move until the food was ready and Ambiades came to nudge me with his boot. "Magus says get up and eat something, O scum of the gutter."

"I heard him," I said as I rolled over and pulled myself to my feet. "Tell me," I said over my shoulder, "O source of all knowledge, have you figured out the difference between a fig tree and an olive?"

He reddened, and I went to eat my dinner satisfied.

After dinner, which was skimpy, the magus pointed to a bed-roll and said it was mine. The sun was still high in the sky. It wouldn't reach the horizon for several hours, but I rearranged the blanket and lay down. There was a heavy cloak to cover me while I slept. I ran my hand across the finely woven wool. It was dark blue on the outside, like the magus's, and was lined with a creamy gold color like a barley field before harvesting. There was no embroidery, but it was carefully made. I would need it as the heat of the day faded. Out of the corner of my eye, I saw the magus watching me finger the wool, like a tailor assessing its value—or like scum from the gutter touching something he knows he shouldn't. I turned my back on him and let him think what he wanted.

The other four continued to sit around the fire. The magus had left plant classification behind and was quizzing his apprentices on history when I fell asleep.

* * *

The next morning before noon we reached a small farmhouse that was sitting in near ruin at the end of the trail. Its whitewash had faded, and its plaster had dropped off in chunks, revealing the lumpy stone walls underneath. A man came to the doorway as we arrived in its weed-grown yard.

"I expected you last night," he said to the magus.

The magus glanced at me. "We moved more slowly than I expected," he said. "Did you get the provisions?"

"Everything," said the man. "There's fodder in the shed for the horses, enough for two weeks, and if you don't come back this way, then I'll take them back down to the city."

"Good enough," said the magus. He opened one of the saddlebags and raised himself on his toes to look inside. He pulled out the leg iron I'd slept in at the inns and then sent Ambiades and Sophos off with the horses. Pol and I followed him into the house, through the empty main room to a back room that had windows on three walls and held several narrow beds.

"It's too late to start up the mountain today," the magus said to Pol as we went in. "We'll stay here and start tomorrow morning. You," he said to me, "should be able to rest to your heart's content." He had me sit on one of the beds and knelt to lock the cuff around my ankle. He tested with two fingers to make sure that it wasn't too tight.

"I forgot to get any padding," he said. "You'll have to live without it until the boys bring in the saddlebags." He looped the chain through the bed frame and pulled on the cuff to make sure that it wouldn't slip off my heel. Then he and Pol went away. I shifted the cuff into a comfortable place and wondered if the dent formed in my ankle would be permanent.

The room was cool, none of its windows faced south, and by the time the magus returned to wrap my ankle in one of Pol's shirts, I was asleep. I spent the day dozing. Sometimes I sat up to look out the window above my bed at the sunlight falling bright and hot outside. Once I saw Pol teaching Ambiades and Sophos to fence with wooden swords, but it could have been a dream; the next time I sat up they were gone.

After dinner I lay and listened to the voices in the other room. The sky grew dark, and the stars came out. I was asleep again before the moon rose and didn't stir until Sophos told me that breakfast was waiting. There was an overfull bowl of cooked oats and another bowl of yogurt as well as bread and cheese and olives and several oranges, the small, lumpy kind that are hard to peel but juicy and sweet.

"Enjoy it," said the magus, seeing that I was. "You won't eat so well again for a while."

I ate what I could and didn't complain about anything. When the magus asked me if I could please not chew with my mouth open, as I had been doing assiduously since our first meal together, I obliged him with a visible effort. Pol worked on my wrists, pulling the stained bandages off, cleaning the blisters, and rubbing more salve into them. I didn't try to wiggle away, and I produced only enough curses to let him know that I could have made more noise but was refraining. The sores were already much better, and I concurred when he decided to leave them exposed to the air for the day, although I could see that it didn't matter if I concurred or not.

It was lucky that I hadn't gotten sick in prison. If I had, it would have taken more than three days of food and fresh air to make me feel so well. While the magus directed the filling of backpacks that everyone but me would carry, I stretched my muscles, bending down to touch my toes, leaning over backward onto my hands, checking to see how much of my strength had returned after a day of rest, and wondering how much longer I had before the magus needed me fit to work. Then I sat on the stone threshold of the house and waited while the others shouldered their burdens.

In front of me the mountains began in earnest. They lifted above their foothills with a rush, their stony slopes dotted with tenacious bushes that had found a hold in loose shale. Sticking out like the bones in ankles and knees were solid outcroppings of limestone and marble. Anyone could see that the rubble piled on top of the steep slopes made the mountains nearly unscalable, the perfect defense for Eddis, the country hidden in the valleys near their summits. There were gorges carved by water, and somewhere there were quarries, but I wasn't sure where to look for them cut into the mountainside, because I wasn't positive where I was myself—somewhere inland of the Seperchia was all I knew for certain.

The magus called me away from my stone threshold and led the way up the hill beside the house to a narrow crevice sliced in the side of the mountain. The trail that had been no wider than a horse the day before was no wider than a man and barely visible. We walked along an old streambed, probably dry for most of the year. When swollen with winter rains, the stream had carved its way through the shale and slate and with more difficulty but just as inevitably through the marble and granite. Where the water flowed the olives had taken root. The mountain walls rose on either side of us, sometimes in solid stone walls several hundred feet high. The red shank and green shank grew in scrubby clumps that left dry scratches on our skin as we brushed by.

When the track occasionally ended in a small cliff that would be a waterfall for the stream in the rainy season, the magus looked for footholds on either side of the streambed and always found them. We ran into no impassable obstacles although we climbed over fallen tree trunks and sometimes scrambled uphill on fingers and toes. I was happy to have my soft-soled boots.

We stopped for lunch before I'd exhausted myself, but I was glad to rest. It was clear that the magus meant to lead us up the streambed until at some point we left Sounis and entered the mountain country, Eddis. Maybe we already had. I hesitated to ask, but I was delighted when Ambiades did.

"Where are we?"

"Eddis, since that last climb."

"Why?"

My eyebrows lifted. So the magus hadn't told his apprentices where we were going. I wondered if he'd told Pol.

The magus turned to Sophos to ask, "What did you learn about Eddis from your tutor?"

So Sophos recited what he knew while we ate our lunch. Eddis was ruled by a queen and a court of eleven ministers, including a prime minister. Its main exports were lumber and silver from mines. It imported most of its grain, olives, and wine. The country was narrow and ran along the top of the mountain ranges to the north and northeast of Sounis.

It sounded like a paragraph from a book describing "All Our Neighbors" or something equally simpleminded.

When Sophos was done, the magus turned to his senior apprentice. "Tell me what you think are the most significant facts about Eddis." And Ambiades performed admirably. It made me think he had some aptitude for his training, though I'd gotten the feeling that he thought his apprenticeship was somehow beneath him. Maybe it rankled that Sophos was the son of a duke and he wasn't.

"Eddis controls the only easily traversable pass through the mountains between Sounis and Attolia, the two wealthiest trading countries in this part of the world. It has the only remaining timber industry on this coast. All of our forests have been logged. They don't have many other natural resources in the mountains and they get most of their wealth as a result of other peoples' trade. Eddis taxes the caravans that go through the mountains and sells her lumber to Attolia and Sounis for merchant ships. Because she depends on trade, she has always been neutral and tried to keep the peace between Attolia and Sounis. After we drove out the invaders, we would have invaded Attolia, but the Eddisians wouldn't let us."

"Very good," said the magus. He turned to Sophos and asked him if he knew about that incident.

"When they took apart the bridge across the Seperchia?" Sophos guessed.

"Yes," said the magus. "It runs through a gorge, and without crossing the gorge, an army can't get down the far side of the pass into Attolia."

"They were cowards, and they knew they were safe in their mountains," said Ambiades. He spoke confidently an opinion held by most Sounisians.

"Why should they have let Sounis through if war would hurt trade?" I asked, forgetting that I risked rebuke by intruding on the conversation of my betters.

Even Sophos knew the answer. "Because the Attolians had lied. Eddis let the Attolians bring an army through the pass when the invaders first came because it was supposed to fight on our side, but instead the army helped the invaders overrun us at the siege of Solonis."

"So after all that time Sounis was out for revenge?" Several hundred years seemed like a long time to nurse a grudge.

"Most people find it galling to lose their freedom, Gen," the magus said dryly. The remark passed over Sophos's head, but Ambiades laughed.

I said, "Yeah, but Eddis didn't get overrun, did it? The invaders never conquered them?"

"No," said the magus. "The invaders eventually overran Attolia as well as Sounis, but the rule of Eddis has never changed hands at the instigation of an outside force." That was the end of the conversation and of lunch. We went back to our ascent.

Twilight came mercifully early in the deep ravine of the streambed. Our party slowed down once we could no longer see to place our feet reliably. Pol helped me along, and I had to take a hand from Ambiades as well. Finally we came to a wider area of the trail and a flat space that had served many travelers as a camping spot. Someone had built a stone fireplace against the wall of the ravine, and the granite above it was blackened by many fires.

After dinner, when our bedrolls were spread out on the ground behind us, we sat around the fire, and Ambiades asked again why we were in Eddis. The magus answered with another question, which Ambiades answered patiently, obviously used to this response to his inquiries.

"What do you know about the rule of succession in Eddis?"

"Well, they have a queen, like Attolia, so the throne can't descend only in the male line. I suppose the rule is passed from parent to child, just like Sounis."

"And do you know if that has always been true?"

Ambiades shrugged. "Since the invaders."

"And before?"

"Are you talking about Hamiathes's Gift?" Ambiades caught on quickly.

"I am," said the magus, and turned to Sophos. "Do you know about the Gift?" Sophos didn't, so the magus explained.

"It's not surprising. Sounis and Attolia long ago converted to the invaders' religion, and we worship those gods in the basilica in the city, but once we all worshiped the gods of the mountain country. There is an almost infinite pantheon with a deity for each spring and river, mountain and forest, but there is a higher court of more powerful gods ruled by Hephestia, goddess of fire and lightning. She governs all the gods except her mother, the Earth, and her father, the Sky.

"The reign of Eddis supposedly arose out of one of the stories in which Hephestia rewarded a king named Hamiathes with a stone dipped in the water of immortality. The stone freed its bearer from death, but at the end of his natural life span the king passed the stone to his son and died. The son eventually passed it to his son, and the possession of it became synonymous with the right to rule the country. When a usurper stole the stone and soon thereafter died, it was understood that the power of the stone was lost unless it was *given* to the bearer, and so a tradition grew up that allowed the throne of Eddis to change hands peacefully when another country might have had a civil war. One person stole the stone and then gave it to his chosen candidate for the throne, in that way making him rightful king."

"But this is just myth," protested Ambiades. I silently agreed with him.

"It's hard to say what is myth and what is real," said the magus. "There may have been a king called Hamiathes, and he may have initiated this tradition. We do know that there was a stone called Hamiathes's Gift and that at the time of the invaders people still believed in its power and its authority. So much so that the invaders attacked Eddis to gain control of the country by gaining control of the stone, which was additionally rumored to be some sort of fabulous gem. When the Gift disappeared, the invaders were thrown back off the mountain and returned their attention to Sounis and Attolia, which were more easily administered countries."

"What had happened to the stone?" asked Sophos.

"It had been hidden by the king of Eddis, and he died without passing it to his son and without revealing its hiding place. It has remained hidden ever since."

"Do you think it could ever be found?" Sophos asked.

The magus nodded. There was a short silence.

"You think *you* can find it?" asked Ambiades, his face pinched with eagerness and probably greed, I thought.

The magus nodded.

"Do you mean," I squawked, "that we are out here in the dark looking for something from a *fairy tale?*"

The magus looked at me. I think he'd forgotten that I was there listening to him lecture his apprentices. "Reliable documents did survive from the time before the invaders, Gen. They mention the stone."

"And you really think you know where it is?" Ambiades persisted.

"Yes."

"Where?" he asked, while I shook my head in disbelief.

"If it really exists, why," I asked, "after hundreds of years are you the first one to locate it?"

"I'm not." The magus's answer surprised me. "According to the records I've found, a number of other people have gone to look for the stone, but those who came closest to where I think it is hidden never came back. This makes me think that in one way at least they were poorly equipped." He smiled benignly at me across the fire. "Traditionally it took an exceptionally talented thief to bring away the stone, and that's why you've been invited to grace our party."

"Would those records you found be the ones you think survived since before the invaders?" Things that old I'd have to see before I believed in them.

"Yes," said the magus, hooking his linked hands over one knee and rocking back and forth in self-congratulation, "although they survive no more. Once I elicited the information I needed, they were destroyed to prevent anyone else from following the same trail."

I winced. It would have been better if the records hadn't been discovered at all. Ambiades asked again where we were going.

"You'll see when we get there," said his master.

"And why are we going?" I asked derisively. "So that you can be king of Eddis? A hopelessly backward country full of woodcutters?" It was the most charitable description of Eddisians that I had heard in the city.

"I will give the stone to Sounis of course. He will be king. I will be the King's Thief."

This pricked my professional pride. I was going to do the stealing, and he was going to take the credit. His name would be carved in stone on a stele outside the basilica, and mine would be written in the dust. I reminded him that it was my place to be King's Thief. "Or do you expect me to hand you Hamiathes's Gift and then get knifed in the back? Is that why you brought Pol?"

He didn't rise to my bait, and Pol didn't so much as shift his weight on the far side of the fire. A little chill ran up my spine.

"That won't be necessary," said the magus coolly. "No one would mistake you for anything but a tool, Gen. If a sword is well made, does the credit go to the blacksmith or to his hammer? How much smarter than a hammer can you be if you flaunt the proof of your crimes in a wineshop?" I flushed, and he laughed. If I hadn't already been angry, it might not have seemed unkind laughter.

"What would you do if you were King's Thief, Gen? Chew with your mouth open in the royal presence? Chat with the court ladies, dropping the *h*'s at the beginning of your words and garbling the ends of most of them? Everything about you reveals your low birth. You'd never be comfortable at the court."

"I'd be *famous*."

"Oh, you're that already, Gen," he said pityingly.

I'd have been amused myself if Ambiades's snicker hadn't rubbed me on the raw. I changed ground.

"And Sounis trusts you to bring the stone back to him?"

"Of course," the magus snapped. I'd hit a sore point. He'd made sure that Sounis had to trust him, destroying all the records so that no one else could locate the stone.

"Are you sure?" I needled him. "Maybe *that's* why Pol is along. Maybe you're the one to be knifed in the back." His eyebrows flattened over his nose. He was angry at last.

"Don't be stupid," he said.

"And why should Sounis be king of Eddis as well? He already has one country," I said. "And all they have up there"—I waved to the mountain behind me—"is trees. A lot of trees. Does he want to build boats?"

"No," the magus explained, remembering that I was hardly worth being angry at, "he wants the queen."

I dropped my mouth open in patent disbelief. "We're doing this so that he can get—"

"—married," said the magus. "Eddis has refused him so far, but she won't be able to if he can show that he is the rightful ruler of her country. We've warned her that at his next proposal he will be the bearer of Hamiathes's Gift." And that's why we were all out in the dark fetching what he had already promised to deliver.

"What if no one believes in your silly Hamiathes's Gift anymore?" I asked. "What if we find it and everyone says, 'So what?'"

"She is not so secure on her throne that she can risk offending her people's gods. No woman could be."

I looked into the fire. For a while there was quiet around the campfire. "He doesn't want the queen," I said at last, the truth forcing its way out. "He doesn't even want the country. He wants the pass through the mountains so that he can invade Attolia."

Pol and Ambiades nodded their heads on the other side of the fire. To anyone who knew Sounis, this explanation made more sense than the one the magus offered.

The magus shrugged. "It's not important why he wants the Gift. What's important is that we get it. And now I think you'd better get some rest."

Like a good tool, for instance, a very well-behaved hammer, I stretched out by the fire and went to sleep.

The next morning light came slowly to the gorge, and I was well rested by the time our day started, but the conversation of the night before still rankled, and I took care to chew with my mouth open at breakfast until the magus winced and looked away. The gorge grew wider, and the olive trees disappeared. We walked past juniper and red shank and green shank bushes and the occasional fir tree as the stone cliffs were replaced by steep hillsides covered with loose rocks. Finally, in the evening, the gorge widened still further, and we were in a narrow valley filled with trees. The path underfoot changed from hard rock to dirt and then to dirt covered with pine needles. We made no sound as we climbed out of the valley into a larger forest that stretched indefinitely in front of us.

"I told you there was nothing up here but trees," I said as I turned around to look at the way we had come. I could see down the cut of the gorge until the trail twisted, and between the mountains I could see all the way out to the plains beyond. The road we had followed to the foothills was not visible, nor was the city, but we could see a bend of the Seperchia twisting across the plain, and beyond that there was a glimpse of the sea.

"Can we stop now?" I wanted to know. "My feet are tired."

"No." The magus shook his head. "Get moving."

Our trail continued between the trees. We made no sound as we walked and walked. I looked up at the branches that blocked any view of the sky overhead, mountain fir, with their cones beginning to open in order to drop their seeds. I said, "This is boring. How come boring makes me so tired?"

When no one answered, I asked again, "When can we stop?"

The magus slowed down to look over his shoulder. "Shut up."

"I just wanted—"

Pol was behind me as usual. He leaned forward to give me a shove in the shoulder blades.

It was almost dark when we came to a road through the forest paved with giant stones laid perfectly evenly. We waited under the trees until the magus was sure that the road was empty, and then we all sped across to the forest on the other side.

"Where does the road go?" Ambiades asked the magus.

"From Eddis's capital city to the main pass through the mountains."

"How did they lay it?" Sophos wanted to know.

The magus shrugged. "It's been too long to know. It was laid at the same time as the old walls of our city. No one knows how it was done."

"Polyfemus," said Ambiades.

"What?" asked Sophos.

"They probably think Polyfemus did it. He was the giant with one eye that supposedly built the old walls of the city and the king's prison. Don't you know any of these stories?"

Sophos shook his head. "My father thinks that we should forget the old gods. He says that a country with two sets of gods is like a country with two kings. No one knows which to be loyal to."

The track continued on the far side of the stone road. We followed it into the trees until the sun set behind a bump of mountain. The twilight lasted while we set up a camp just off the trail and Pol made dinner on a small cookfire. The pine needles provided easy kindling.

While we ate, I picked at the magus. I liked to watch him lose his temper and then regain it when he remembered that I was supposed to be beneath his contempt. When he and Pol tried to plan how to make up the day we had lost at the mountain house, I told him that if he had wanted to move faster, he should have had a cart for the early stage of the trip. Before I was done with my dinner, I asked for seconds and complained that he should have brought more food. I talked with my mouth full.

"You don't have to carry it," Ambiades pointed out.

"Yes," said the magus. "Maybe we should have you carry your own share tomorrow?"

"Oh, no, not me," I said. "I'm worn out just hauling myself up here." I lay down on my bedroll and wriggled on my backside until I could put my feet up on the trunk of a fallen tree. "Why didn't you bring something more comfortable to sleep on?"

The magus started to answer, but Sophos interrupted. He asked the magus to tell him more about the old gods of Eddis.

"I thought your father didn't want you to hear about them," said Ambiades.

Sophos thought for a minute. "I think he just doesn't want people to believe in them, to have superstitions. I don't think he objects to an academic interest."

"He doesn't?" Ambiades laughed. "I thought an academic interest was exactly what he objected to. Didn't he threaten to throw you into the river tied to a stack of encyclopedias?"

Even Pol laughed as Sophos blushed. "He doesn't think I should spend so much time on book learning, but he thinks it's all right for other people."

There was a little silence at the fireside that I didn't understand. To judge by the look on Ambiades's face, whatever it was that bothered him had come upon him with a vengeance. To fill the silence, the magus told Sophos he would teach him some stories of the old gods. He began with the creation and the birth of the gods, and he didn't do such a poor job. I lay on my back and listened.

chapter 5

## earth's creation
## and the birth
## of the gods

Earth was alone. She had no companion. So she took a piece
from the center of herself and made the sun and that was the
first god. But in time he left Earth. He promised to always
send her light during the day, but at night she was still alone.
So she took a piece from the edge of herself and made the
moon, and she was the first goddess. After a while the moon
too went away from Earth. She promised to send her light to
keep Earth company at night, but the moon's promises are
worth nothing, and she sent only part of her light and
sometimes forgot entirely. When she forgot, there was no
moonlight at all, and the Earth was lonely again.

So she breathed out into the firmament, and she made the
Sky. The Sky wrapped himself all around her and was her

companion. He promised to stay with her always, and Earth was happy Earth and the Sky's first children were the mountain ranges, and Hephestia was the oldest. They had more children who were the great oceans and the middle sea, and their youngest children were the great rivers Seperchia and Skander.

One day the Sky wanted to know what he looked like, so the Earth made a thousand goddesses and spread them all across the world to hold mirrors for the sky, and those are the lakes. The Sky looked at himself in the mirrors. He was blue and white with clouds and sometimes black and spangled with stars, and when the sun set, he was beautiful indeed. He grew vain. He looked at the Earth, who was round and colorless, and he felt superior.

"I am quite beautiful," he said to Earth, "but you are very dull. The only pretty things about you are your lakes." And he spent all his time looking into the water and would not speak to Earth. So Earth swept up the dust from the mountains and made snow and the dust from the valleys and made dark black soil, and in the soil she scattered the seeds for forests and flowers and covered herself with green trees and bright colors and told the Sky that she was as beautiful as he. But he had eyes only for the lakes, who reflected his own glory. They bore him children, who were the smaller rivers and streams. Earth was jealous and made trees grow up around each of the lakes, hiding them from the Sky's view.

The Sky was angry. He took up some of the black soil from Earth's valleys and some of the snow from her mountains, and he mixed them together and blew hard and scattered them across the world. Every speck of dust grew into a human, some dark like the valley soil and some white as the snow. So, though we come from the Earth, we must thank the Sky for our creation, because it was the Sky that made man. But he was impatient and did not do such a job as the Earth would have done. Man came out small and weak and without the gifts of the gods. When the Sky sent men to clear the forest around the lakes, that he might see them, they were too weak to pull down the trees.

Earth looked at them climbing through her forests and said, "Why have you made these?"

And the Sky was ashamed, and he told her that he wanted to see the lakes, and the Earth was ashamed and said that she wanted the Sky to speak only to her. The Sky promised that he would look at the lakes only sometimes, and the Earth promised to hide only some of the lakes in the trees. And they were happy.

But Earth watched the humans that the Sky had made and felt sorry for them. They were cold and hungry. So she gave them fire to make them warm, and she gave them seeds to scatter on the ground. She made animals for them to eat, but no matter what gifts she gave them the humans were ungrateful. They thanked only the Sky for having made them. The Earth grew angry and she shook with her anger, and the houses that the humans had built fell down and the animals that they had gathered were frightened and ran away, and the humans realized that they had made a terrible mistake. From then on there were always some humans who thanked the Earth for her gifts and some humans who thanked the Sky for their creation.

When the magus was finished, the group of us sitting around the fire was quiet. Then Sophos asked, "The people in Eddis, do they really believe that?"

I barked with laughter, and everyone looked at me. "In the

city of Sounis do they really believe that the Nine Gods won the Earth in a battle with Giants? That the First God spawns godlets left and right and his wife is a shrew who is always outwitted?" I lifted the back of my head off the ground and crossed my arms underneath it. "No, they don't believe that, Sophos. It's just religion. They like to go up to the temple on feast days and pretend that there is some god who wants the worthless sacrificial bits of a cow, and people get to eat the rest. It's just an excuse to kill a cow."

"You sound very learned, Gen. What do you know about it?" asked the magus.

I sat up and moved to the fire before I answered him. "My mother was from the mountain country. It's no different there. Everybody goes to the temple, and everybody likes to hear the old stories after dinner, but that doesn't mean they expect a god to show up at their door."

"Oh?"

"Yes," I said, letting my tongue run away from me. "And you made a lot of mistakes. You aren't even pronouncing the name of the country right. The people on the mountains call it Eeddis, not Eddis. And you left out the part where the Earth cries when the Sky God ignores her and turns the oceans to salt."

"I did?"

"Yes, I told you, my mother told me the stories when I was little. I know them all, and I know that they call the country Eeddis."

"As for that, Gen, I can tell you that Eeddis is the old pronunciation used before the invaders came. We've changed the pronunciation of many of our words since the time of the invaders, while Eddisian pronunciations haven't altered for centuries. *Eddis* is pronounced differently now, whatever the people of that country say."

"It's their country," I grumbled. "They ought to know the right name for it."

"It isn't that Eeddis is the wrong name, Gen. It's just an old way of saying the same word. The rest of the civilized world has moved on. Tell me what other mistakes I made."

I told him as many as I'd noticed. Most of the mistakes were bits of the story that he had left out.

When I was done, he said, "It's always interesting to hear different versions of people's folktales, Gen, but you shouldn't think that your mother's stories are true to the original ones. I've studied them for many years and am sure that I have the most accurate versions. It often happens that emigrants like your mother can't remember parts of the original, so they make things up and then forget that the story was ever different. Many of these myths were created by great storytellers centuries ago, and it is inevitable that in the hands of common people they get debased."

"My mother never debased anything in her entire life," I said hotly.

"Oh, don't be offended," the magus said. "I'm sure she never meant to, but your mother wasn't educated. Uneducated people rarely know much about the things they talk about every day. She probably never even knew that your name, Gen, comes from the longer name Eugenides."

"She did, too," I insisted. "You're the one that doesn't know anything. You never knew my mother, and you don't know anything about her."

"Don't be silly. Of course I know about her. She fell from a fourth-story window of Baron Eructhes's villa and died when you were ten years old."

The wind sighed in the pine needles over my head. I'd forgotten that that was written in the pamphlet that was my criminal record. The king's courts were apt to have a pickpocket's entire life story written in tiny handwriting on a collection of paper sheets folded together in the prison's record room

The magus saw that he had cut deep and went on. His voice dripped condescension. "Maybe I'm wrong. Maybe Gen is a family name. The title of King's Thief is a hereditary one now in Eddis, and I think the current Thief is named Eugenides. Maybe you're related. A cousin, perhaps, to someone exalted." He snickered. I could feel my face burning and knew that I was red right to the hairline.

"Eugenides," I nearly stuttered, "was the god of thieves. We are *all* named after him." I jumped up from the fire and stamped back to the blanket that was mine. The night was cool, so I wrapped up in the wool cloak and admitted to myself that the magus had gotten the better of me in that exchange. Everyone else seemed to agree.

The magus was as smug as a cat the next day. Pol made breakfast, and then we packed up, careful to leave no sign of our presence beside the trail. Sophos and Ambiades collected pine needles to cover the burnt space of our cooking fire. By noon we had reached the other side of the mountain ridge and were looking at our descent.

"I am not going down that until I've had lunch," I announced. "I have no intention of dying on an empty stomach." I was flip but perfectly serious, and when the magus tried to force me, I balked. He cuffed me on the head with his seal ring, but I wouldn't budge. I was going to rest before I started down a shale slope where I would need not only my balance but all the strength that the king's prison had left in my legs. I dug in my heels and wouldn't move. We had lunch.

After lunch we started down the mountainside. I wanted to go last, but Pol wouldn't let me. I went second to last and only had to worry about the rocks that Pol kicked down. The magus, who went first, had Pol's rocks as well as mine, Sophos's, and Ambiades's. I sent down a few especially for him but felt bad when Sophos caught one of the rocks that Pol kicked loose squarely in the back of the head. None of us could stop to see if he was badly hurt until we'd reached the end of the flysch. It was about seventy-five feet to the bottom of it, and as soon as we were safely on solid rock, Pol checked Sophos.

"Turn around," he said.

"It's all right," said Sophos, but his eyes were still watering. "It's not bleeding." He kept looking at his hand to be sure. Pol rubbed the bump rising on the back of his head and agreed that he would probably live.

"I regret that," he said, and seemed very serious about his apology for something he could not have prevented. "Do you need to rest for a while?"

"We could have a second lunch," I suggested, and received a glare from the magus.

Sophos said he was fine, so we started again. There was no streambed here to follow, at least not at first. We walked across the side of the mountain on a goat path between rocks. I felt very exposed and worried about who might be watching from above. The last thing I wanted was to be caught hiking across Eddis with the king's magus of Sounis, and we could not have been more visible, five people traipsing through vegetation no higher than our knees. I asked the magus why the secrecy in the morning when anyone passing could see us in the open.

"Only someone else on this trail," he said. "And the trail is rarely used. As long as we don't leave any permanent signs, no one will know that we passed here. There are better ways to get down to Attolia."

I looked up at the rubble above and said, "I bet there are. Can't we be seen from the forest?"

"No, it's unlikely that anyone would be there."

I snorted. "A successful thief doesn't depend on things being *unlikely* to happen," I said.

"A successful thief?" said the magus. "How would you know?"

I retired chagrined from the field of contest.

After a quarter of a mile we picked our way down a particularly steep slope and came to a tiny plateau, paved with flagstones and edged with ancient olive trees. At the back of the plateau, really no more than a deep ledge, a cave led into the mountainside. Growing out of a cleft in the stone above the cave, a fig tree shaded its opening. A spring welled up somewhere in the dark and ran out through a tiled channel in the pavement. Beside the channel was a tiny temple, no more than ten feet high, built from blocks of marble, with miniature marble pillars in front.

"Behold," said the magus with a sweep of his hand, "the place where we were supposed to have lunch. Take a quick look, Sophos. It's your first heathen temple." He explained that it was an altar to the goddess of the spring that rose in the cave. It had probably been built as much as a thousand years earlier. He showed him the craftsmanship that went into dressing the marble, so that each stone fit perfectly against the others.

"Looking at a small temple like this, you can see how the larger temples were fitted together. Everything is in scale. If there are four pieces to each column in the main temple of the river gods, then there are four pieces to each column here, and all the joining will be the same." Sophos was as fascinated as the magus. The two of them went into the temple to see the figure of the goddess and came out looking impressed. Ambiades was bored.

The magus saw his expression and said, "So, Ambiades, knowing someone's religion can help you manipulate that person, which is why Sophos's father thinks no country should have more than one set of gods. Let me give you some examples."

We started down the path that the water from the spring had carved during the last millennium. It was an easy hike. There were even steps carved into the stone at the steep places, no doubt by a thousand years of worshipers at the shrine above us. As we walked, Ambiades listened with interest to the magus. It was obvious that he paid close attention to anything that he thought might be useful to him. He just didn't see the point in natural history.

The magus began to ask questions. For a long time Ambiades answered each one; then Sophos began answering, and Ambiades's comments became more and more sullen. I tried to listen, but only bits and pieces floated back up the trail. After Ambiades had snarled at Sophos a few times, the magus sent Sophos to walk in the back and lectured to Ambiades alone. I was surprised to hear Sophos and Pol behind me chatting like old friends. Pol wanted to know what had set off Ambiades.

"Identifying mountain ranges. He doesn't like that sort of thing, so he doesn't pay attention. But even so, he knows more than I do."

"You'll catch up."

"I suppose, if my father lets me stay."

"Oh?"

"You know what I mean, Pol. If he finds out I want to stay, he'll take me away."

"And do you want to stay?"

"Yes," said Sophos quite firmly. "I like learning, and the magus isn't as frightening as I thought at first."

"No? Shall I tell him you said so?"

"Don't you dare. And don't tell my father either. You know my father is hoping he'll toughen me up. Don't you think the magus is nicer than he seems at first?"

"I couldn't say," said Pol.

"Well, he isn't nearly as hard on me as he is on Ambiades."

"Leaves that to Ambiades, I notice," said Pol.

"Oh, I don't mind, Pol. I like Ambiades. He's smart, and he's not usually so . . . so—"

"High-handed?" Pol supplied the word.

"Temperamental," said Sophos. "I think something is bothering him." He changed the subject. "Do you know where we're going?"

I pricked up my ears.

"Attolia," said Pol, which was nothing more than the obvious at that point.

"Is that all you know? Then why are you here?"

"Your father sent me to keep an eye on you. Toughen you up."

Sophos laughed. "No, really, why?"

"Just what I said."

"I'll bet the magus needed someone reliable, and Father said he couldn't have you without me."

I bet he was right.

We came to a steep place and had to scramble. Once we'd worked our way down, Pol dropped behind Sophos, effectively ending their conversation. Sophos moved up beside me.

"Are you really named after the god of thieves?"

"I am."

"Well, how could they tell what you were going to be when you were just a baby?"

"How did they know what you were going to be when you were a baby?"

"My father was a duke."

"So my mother was a thief."

"So you would have to grow up to be one, too?"

"Most of the people in my family thought so. My father wanted me to be a soldier, but he's been disappointed."

Behind us I heard Pol grunt. He no doubt thought my father's disappointment was justified.

"Your father? He did?"

Sophos sounded so surprised that I looked over at him and asked, "Why shouldn't he?"

"Oh, well, I mean . . ." Sophos turned red, and I wondered about the circulation of his blood; maybe his body kept an extra supply of it in his head, ready for blushing.

"What surprises you?" I asked. "That my father was a soldier? Or that I knew him? Did you think that I was illegitimate?"

Sophos opened and closed his mouth without saying anything.

I told him that no, I wasn't illegitimate. "I even have brothers and sisters," I told him, "with the same father." Poor Sophos looked as if he wanted the ground to swallow him.

"What do they do?" he finally asked.

"Well, one of my brothers is a soldier, and the other brother is a watchmaker."

"Really? Can he make those new watches that are flat instead of round in the back?" He seemed interested, and I was going to tell him that Stenides had made his first flat watch about two years ago, but the magus noticed Sophos talking to me and called him away.

As Sophos pulled ahead, I said loudly, "My sisters are even married, and honest housewives to boot." At least they were mostly honest.

The valley eroded by the spring never deepened enough to be called a gorge. Its sides curved gently away from us, and only in a few places was the going stony. As we descended, we could see Attolia stretched out ahead of us, and to the right the sea. Dotted across the horizon, islands continued the mountain range behind us. On the far side of the Attolian valley was another mountain range, and out of that came the Seperchia River. It wandered along the plain, sometimes nearer to the Hephestial Mountains, sometimes many miles away. Just before it reached the coast, it bumped against a rocky spur of the foothills and was diverted into the Hephestial range itself. There the mountains were soft limestone, and the river had cut a pass down to Sounis to flow past the king's city and finally into the middle sea.

"It's much greener than home, isn't it?" Sophos commented to no one in particular.

He was quite right. Where the view of Sounis had been brown and baked gold, this country was shades of green. Even the olive trees, planted below us, were a richer color than the silver gray trees on the other side of the range.

"They get the easterly winds that dump their rain when they hit the mountains," the magus explained. "Attolia gets nearly twice as much rain every year as we do."

"They export wine, figs, olives, and grapes as well as cereals. They have pastureland to support their own cattle, and they don't import sheep from Eddis," Ambiades said knowledgeably, and the magus laughed.

"Gods, you were paying attention!"

I thought at first that Ambiades was going to smile, but he scowled instead and didn't speak until we stopped for the night, and then it was only to berate Sophos. It was strange behavior for someone who had been so contented by the fire the night before. I couldn't see why Sophos liked him, but it was obvious that he did. Worshiped might be a better word. All he needed to do was build a miniature temple and get Ambiades to stand on the altar.

I guessed that Ambiades was usually more pleasant company. The magus didn't seem likely to tolerate prolonged sullenness in an apprentice, and it seemed to me that he thought highly of Ambiades even if he did call him a fool from time to time.

After dinner Sophos asked if there were other stories about the gods, and the magus began the story of Eugenides and the Sky God's Thunderbolts but stopped almost immediately.

"He's your patron god," he said to me. "Why don't you tell Sophos who he is?"

I don't know what he expected me to say, but I told the entire story as I had learned it from my mother, and he didn't interrupt.

## the birth
## of eugenides,
## god of thieves

It had been many years since the creation of man, and he had multiplied across the land. One day as Earth walked through her forests, she met a woodcutter. His axe lay beside him on the ground, and he wept.

"Why weep, woodcutter?" Earth asked him. "I see no hurt."

"Oh, Lady," said the woodcutter, "my hurt is overwhelming because it is someone else's pain that makes me cry."

"What pain?" asked Earth, and the woodcutter explained that he and his wife wished to have children, but they had none, and this made his wife so sad that she sat in her house and wept. And the woodcutter, when he thought of his wife's tears, wept, too.

Earth brushed the tears from his cheeks and told him to meet her again in the forest in nine days, and in that time she would bring him a son.

The woodcutter went home and told his wife what had happened, and in nine days he went again into the forest to meet the goddess there. She asked, "Where is your wife?"

The woodcutter explained that she hadn't come. It is one thing to meet the Goddess in the forest and another thing to convince your wife that you have done so. His wife thought her husband had lost his mind, and she wept all the more.

"Go," said Earth, "and tell your wife to come tomorrow, or she will have no child and no husband and no home either when the day is done."

So the woodcutter went home to his wife and pleaded with her to come to the forest, and to please him, she agreed. So the next day she was with her husband, and Earth asked her, "Have you a cradle?"

And the woman said no. It is one thing to humor your husband, who has suddenly gone crazy, but it is something else to let all the neighbors know that he is crazy by asking to borrow a cradle for a baby he says that you are going to get from the Goddess.

"Go," said Earth, "and get a cradle and small clothes and blankets, or you will have no child and no husband and no home by this time tomorrow."

So the woodcutter and his wife went to their neighbors, and the neighbors were good people. They gave to the woodcutter and his wife the things they said they needed, and they asked no questions because it was perfectly clear to them that their neighbors had lost their wits.

The next day in the forest when Earth asked, "Have you a cradle?" the woodcutter and his wife said, "Yes."

"Have you small clothing?"

They said, "Yes."

"And blankets? And all the things you will need for a baby?" and they said yes, and Earth showed them the baby in her arms. And the woodcutter's wife came close to her, and she said, "Have you a name for him?"

And the Earth had no name. The gods know themselves and have no need of names. It is man who names all things, even gods.

"Then we will call him Eugenides," said the woodcutter's wife, "the wellborn."

They took Eugenides to their home, and he was their own son. The Earth sometimes came in the guise of an old woman and brought him presents. When he was very little, the presents were little, a top that spun in different colors, soap bubbles that hung over his cradle, a blanket of fine moleskin to keep him warm in the winter. When he was five, she brought him the gift of languages that he might understand the animals all around him. When he was ten, she brought him the gift of summoning that he might converse with the lesser gods of streams and lakes.

When Eugenides was fifteen and Earth would have given him immortality, the Sky stopped her on her way.

"Where are you going?" he asked.

"To see my son," said Earth.

"What son have you but mine?" said the Sky.

"I have my own son and the woodcutter's," said Earth, and the Sky was angry. He went to the home of Eugenides and he threw down thunderbolts and the house was destroyed and Eugenides and his parents ran frightened into the forest. The

Sky looked for them there, but the forest was Earth's and in Earth's name hid them.

The Sky grew still more angry and shouted at the Earth, "You shall have no sons but my sons! You shall have no people but my people!" And he threw down his thunderbolts on the villages where the people thanked the Earth for her gifts, but he spared the villages where the people thanked him for their creation.

And the Earth grew angry also and she said she would have none of his people and she shook with her anger and she destroyed the villages that the Sky God had spared. All over the world the villages of the Earth's people and the Sky's people were destroyed and the crops burnt in the fields and the animals lost and the people were afraid and prayed for rescue, but Earth and the Sky were too angry to hear them.

All the people in the world might have died then, but Hephestia heard their cries. She was the oldest child of the Earth and the Sky and closest to them in power. She went to each and spoke to them and said, "Why should the Earth not have what children she pleases? Look at the children you have had." And the Sky remembered his children who were streams and rivers and saw that they were choked with refuse of the burning caused by his thunderbolts.

Hephestia went to Earth and said, "Why should you not have the people of the Sky? Look what people you have for your own." And Earth looked and she saw her people afraid, without homes or food, their houses destroyed and all their livelihoods gone. The Sky's people were frightened, too, and they begged her to put away her anger and forgive them if they had offended her. And Earth did put away her anger, and the Sky did put away his anger as well.

Hephestia asked them, "Why should they suffer because

you are angry with each other? Give me your thunderbolts, Father, and give up to me your power to shake the ground, Mother, so that they will not suffer again from your anger with each other."

Earth gave Hephestia her power to shake the ground, and the Sky promised to give her his thunderbolts. He promised also not to harm Eugenides, but he said the Earth must not give him any more presents and never give immortality to any children but his children. Earth promised, and she and the Sky were at peace.

The people of the Sky and the Earth rebuilt their homes and recovered their animals and replanted their fields, but from then on they were careful to build two altars in every village to thank the Sky for their creation and the Earth for her gifts, that they would always be the people of them both. And in times of great need they pray not only to the Earth and the Sky but to Hephestia as well that she will intercede on their behalf with her parents.

"You sound very different when you are telling a story," said Sophos.

"That," I said acidly, "is the way my mother told it to me."

"I liked it."

"Well, it is the only one you will hear tonight," said the magus. "Eugenides and the Sky God will have to wait for tomorrow." To me he said, "Your mother seems to have taken the story and made it her own."

"Of course," jeered Ambiades. "She was a thief."

That night I slept lightly for the first time since being in prison. I woke as the moon, half full, shone on the hillside. I rolled over to look at what stars I could see and noticed Ambiades, sitting up in his blankets.

"What are you doing awake?" I asked him.

"Keeping an eye on you."

I looked at the other three sleeping bodies. "You take turns?" Ambiades nodded.

"Since when?"

"Since the last inn."

"Really? And I've been too tired to appreciate it until now." I shook my head with regret and went back to sleep.

chapter 6

IN THE MORNING we ate the last of the food and drank the last of the water that the others had carried in leather sacks over the mountain. The bread was stale and rock hard, and I wasn't the only one who was hungry when we were through. The magus saw me looking in distaste at the lump of bread in my hand, and he laughed. He was in a cheery mood and seemed willing to set aside our differences since he'd put me thoroughly in my place.

"I know," he said. "Don't bother to complain. I'll get you fresh bread for lunch, I promise."

"How long until lunch?"

He turned to look at the trail ahead of us. It dropped steeply and gave us a view of the valley ahead of us. It was a more limited view than the one we had had higher up the mountain. The river had disappeared. So had the sea. "Can you see that break in the olives?" the magus asked. I looked where he pointed and saw the rooftops of a few houses, only three or four miles away. "We'll get our lunch from there."

"Then I will leave the rest of my breakfast for the birds." I pitched the bread over the rocks around our campsite. Everyone but Pol did the same. As a soldier he had probably eaten worse things.

Soon we were once again in the open. The shallow groove carved by the stream ended at the top of a cliff that was the precipitous edge of the mountain. Sixty feet below whispered waves of olives. Between the cliff and the trees, like the foam left by breaking waves, were jumbled rocks of all sizes. To my left and to my right, the cliff, the trees, and the swirling rocks continued as far as I could see. Ahead, the olives rolled out for miles, rising a little but mostly falling away toward the hidden river, their silver surface broken by islands of shiny green, which were the dry oaks, and by lightning catchers that were lone cypress trees standing like swords on their hilts. The rooftops of the town that the magus had pointed out earlier were the only man-made things to break the surface of the trees.

"It's like a sea," Sophos said, echoing my thoughts.

"It is a sea," said the magus quietly. "It's called the Sea of Olives. It was planted to honor one of the old gods so long ago that no one knows which one. The trees stretch from the coast all the way to the edge of the dystopia, about thirty-five miles inland."

Ambiades was interested in more practical knowledge. "How do we get down?"

I looked around for the goat path that I knew must be around, and I whistled when I found it. "Glad we had a good night's rest," I said. "Everybody did get plenty of sleep, didn't they?" Nobody mentioned standing a three-hour watch.

"Well, dithering won't help," I said.

The path began in a crevasse left behind when a large rock had broken loose from the bluff and dropped to the ground below. There was a shelf about eight feet below the top of the cliff. I flexed my knees and jumped before the magus could stop me. Pol jumped after me and landed so close that he nearly knocked both of us down the slope. I steadied him and called up to Sophos.

"Come on, you're next. Lie down and slide your legs over the lip." Pol and I grabbed him by the legs and lowered him. Once he was down with us, the hollow was filled with bodies. I started the next phase of the descent and left Pol to help the magus and Ambiades.

There was no loose rubble to kick down, or I wouldn't have gone first, but I did worry that one of the others was going to slide down on my head. I went as fast as I safely could.

The path switched back and forth across the cliff, turning every ten feet or so and dropping five feet with each turn. It was only about six inches wide, less in spots, and was more a groove carved into the stone cliff than anything else. There were two bits so steep that I sat down and slithered, grabbing a passing plant to slow down. As I went down, I muttered under my breath, mimicking the magus's voice. "'This trail isn't used much,' he says. 'There are better ones.' I'll bet there are," I said, and swore out loud as my foot slipped. I recovered my balance easily but banged my wrist against an outcropping and swore again.

I sucked on the sore spot as I skittered down the last part of the path and picked my way through the rubble at the bottom. The boulders there were huge, higher than my head, and rested on mounds of smaller rocks that they had dragged down with them when they pulled loose from the cliff face. Once I reached the open space beyond the rocks, I waited for the others. They were slow.

All four of them crabbed along the cliff, holding on with both hands. Even nearly empty, the packs they carried threatened to overbalance everyone but Pol. He and the magus kept stopping to look over their shoulders at me. I looked over my own shoulder and almost went to sit in the shade of the olive trees, but the magus had been more civil than usual, and I wanted to keep him in a good mood. So I waited in the sunlight where he could see me. It was a hot day already, and the sweat trickled down the side of my face.

When everyone else had made it safely down, we moved into the shade and sat down to rest. It was dark under the olives, and cool. The trees were so old and twisted and their leaves grew so thickly that they allowed very little light to reach the ground. Instead of juniper and sage growing underneath them, there was almost nothing, some thin grass, a very few spindly bushes.

"I am going to walk into town to buy horses and lunch," said the magus as he stood up and dusted himself off. "It will take me almost an hour to walk there and back, in addition to the time it takes to buy the horses and provisions. We're still a day behind schedule, so we'll have to eat while we go." He disappeared between the olive trees.

Pol turned where he sat and opened the pack he'd been leaning against. "No need to waste the time we have," he said, and pulled two wooden swords out of the pockets sewn to the outside. He handed one to Sophos and one to Ambiades, and they began their fencing lesson. I remembered the scene that I had watched from the window of the mountain hut, and I supposed that it had not been a dream after all.

"Swords up," said Pol, and they began drills with which they were obviously familiar. Once they had bent and twisted for a while and their muscles were prepared, Pol matched Ambiades and Sophos against each other. They sparred carefully, and I

watched with interest. Ambiades was by far the better swordsman, but then he was four or five years older. Sophos was
just learning the motions, but he showed some talent and coordi-
nation. With a good instructor, he'd be a dangerous opponent.
For now he was too short and too unfamiliar with his weapon
to do anything except wave it around and hope it connected.
At critical moments he occasionally closed his eyes. When
Ambiades leaned in over his guard and whacked him on the
head, I winced.

"Are you all right?" Ambiades dropped his sword, looking concerned. "I thought that you would block that." He put his hand
up to rub Sophos's head, but Pol pushed him back.

"He should have. Try it again." He made Ambiades repeat the
move over and over until Sophos worked out for himself a block
that would come naturally. Sophos got banged twice more on
the head, although Ambiades only hit him lightly. He apologized
each time, and I began to think that under the pride and prickles
there might be a reason to like him. Finally, when Ambiades
rode over the top of Sophos's guard for the seventh or eighth
time, Sophos stepped to one side and blocked the attack from
there.

"Good enough," said Pol, high praise indeed, and ended the
lesson. Sophos and Ambiades threw themselves down in the
grass, panting while Pol put their wooden swords away. I
checked to see that there were pockets sewn to each of their
packs, and the magus's as well. It explained why they hadn't
taken the packs off and tossed them down the cliff before climbing down themselves. Nobody wants his valuable short sword
dropped onto a pile of rocks. I was reassured to know that we
hadn't come into the wilderness armed only with Pol's sword,
but I wondered what the Uselesses, elder and younger, would
do with theirs if we ever got into a fight. I also wondered if

hidden in Pol's pack or the magus's was a gun. Acting on the king's business, they were entitled to carry one, at least in Sounis. Guns weren't as accurate as crossbows, but they were less awkward to transport, and to have one would have been a comfort.

When the swords were back in their packs, Pol settled down on the grass himself and looked expectantly at Sophos.

"Don't match your weakness against your opponent's strength?" Sophos said hesitantly.

"And your weakness is?"

"My height?"

"And Ambiades's strength is?"

"Years of fencing lessons," I said under my breath, but no one heard me.

Sophos gave the correct answer. "His height."

"Remember that."

Then he praised Ambiades mildly and offered him a few tips. He and Ambiades talked like men for a few minutes about sword fighting. Pol clearly respected the things Ambiades had to say, and Ambiades looked pleased and content. I almost liked him myself.

We still had time to wait for the magus, so I lay down on the soft dirt under an olive tree and closed my eyes. When the magus arrived, we were all, except Pol, sleeping. I woke when I heard the horses thumping toward us but didn't move. It was pleasant to lie and look up at the twisted branches and tightly packed leaves of the olive trees. The dirt under my fingertips was powder soft. There was a breeze that moved the smallest branches, and the tiny bits of sky that showed through were white in the midday heat. Flies buzzed around my head. The only other sound was that of the horses' hooves getting closer. It didn't occur to me until the last minute that it might be a stranger and not the magus at all. I nearly jumped out of my skin, but there had been no need to worry.

"Glad to see someone is alert, if a little bit late," said the magus as he walked between the trees. Ambiades and Sophos scrambled up and took the horses, while the magus talked to Pol.

"I think we'll ride down to the road and follow it. We won't reach Profactia until nightfall, and we can cut around it through the trees. There's a moon tonight, and we should be able to stay on the road until quite late. We'll make up some of the time we've lost."

Pol nodded and got up. He helped the Uselesses pack the provisions the magus had brought into the saddlebags. Then we all mounted up and rode slowly between the trees while we ate fresh bread and cheese and more olives. We kept having to lean close to our horses' necks as they walked under branches without caring whether their riders would fit under the branches as well. Donkeys would not have been so tedious. Donkeys, however, would have been left behind once we reached the road.

We moved quickly. I was still hungry but quit eating. It was too much bother to go on holding the horse with one hand while eating with the other. With Pol on one side of me and Ambiades on the other, I bounced up the road until I got used to the feeling. The magus had cautioned Ambiades and Sophos to keep their mouths shut when we were within earshot of other travelers, as their accents would mark them as members of Sounis's upper class.

"You don't need to worry, Gen," he said to me, teasing again.

"Really?"

"Attolian gutter is indistinguishable from Sounisian gutter," he said, and I laughed with the others. I was very content with my slang and my half-swallowed words.

When we were alone on the road, walking the horses for a while to rest them, Sophos asked what would happen if anyone guessed we were not from Attolia.

"Nothing." The magus shrugged. "Traders still do business here. Trade would go on right up until there was open war; it might not stop even then."

"And if they knew *why* we were here?" I asked.

The magus gave me a sharp look before he answered, "They'd probably arrest us and turn us over to their queen." I gathered that he wanted to leave the rest unsaid.

"And she would?" I prompted anyway.

"Behead us all. Publicly."

I shivered and rubbed the back of my neck with one hand. Ambiades looked positively green. He was touchy and unpleasant the rest of the day.

It was twilight and traffic was increasing when we approached Profactia. We dawdled until there was no one in sight on the road and then disappeared into the olive groves, where we waited again until Pol and the magus agreed that all of the olive harvesters would have left the trees for the night. We rode quietly through the trees and saw nothing of the town. I was a little disappointed. We returned to the road without being seen. The moon was up. The night air was cool, and we'd pulled our cloaks out of the saddlebags. We stayed close to the trees like robbers and went on until I was almost worn out. Just as the moon was setting, the magus finally turned his horse into the trees to look for a camping site. We ate our dinner cold and slept without a fire.

Pol woke us before dawn, and the magus led us deeper among the trees, following the guidance of his compass in its brown leather case. After an hour or so, when the sun was beginning to be warm, we stopped for breakfast in a tiny open space where several olive trees had died and not been replaced. Breakfast was just bread and more cheese, but Pol boiled water over a tiny fire and made coffee that was thick with sugar. "That will wake us up," he said.

There was a small spring nearby, and the magus suggested we have a wash before we packed up. Sophos, the magus, and Pol shucked their clothes and splashed ankle deep into the chilly water. After a few hesitations I joined them. I didn't want them to think I liked being clean, but the cool water was refreshing. Only Ambiades remained on the bank, still wrapped in his cloak while his small cup of coffee cooled in front of him. He'd been quiet all morning and, I realized, quiet the evening before—no taunts for me and no gibes for Sophos. He wasn't thinking about a bath in the spring, and I was wondering what unpleasant thoughts were on his mind when he jumped like a startled cat. The magus had flicked cold water on him.

"Come wash," the magus said, and Ambiades stood up and dropped his cloak beside the others on the stream bank. It lay next to Sophos's and made a very poor showing. The other cloaks were well made but ordinary. Mine was probably one of the magus's old ones cut down, and Pol's was a plain military cloak, but Sophos's was a particularly fine specimen, made of expensive fabric generously cut with a stylish silk tassel hanging from the hem at the back. Beside it, the narrow cut of Ambiades's cloak was flashy but out of fashion, and there was a line of holes, poorly darned, that ran from neck to hem, where a moth had been eating it during its summer storage.

As he dabbled his toes in the water, Ambiades looked over at the magus and Sophos, who were already stepping out of the stream, finished with their quick wash. His eyes narrowed, and the hair on the back of my neck started to rise. I've seen envy before, and I know the damage it can do. Ambiades caught me staring, and his envy was replaced by righteous contempt. If one thing was perfectly clear to him, it was my worthless place in the universe.

"What are you looking at, sewer filth?" he snarled.

"The Lord of Rags and Tatters," I said with a false smile as I bowed elaborately and gestured to his ratty cloak.

A moment later I was on my back in the cold water of the stream with the sun in my eyes and my ears ringing. Ambiades stood over me shouting something about his grandfather's having been the duke of somewhere. He would have kicked me, but Pol was there and put a hand on his shoulder to pull him back. A moment later the magus was standing between me and the sun.

"A little circumspection might be wise for someone in your position, Gen," he said mildly. "Not to mention an apology."

Well, my position was not a good one, I was willing to admit, but it was easily changed. I pulled my knees up to my chest and rolled myself onto my feet. "Apologize?" I said to the magus. "What for?" I walked away, nursing my swelling lip and licking the blood from the corner of my mouth. I paused to filch a comb from an open saddle pack and then sat on the stump of a dead olive to get the tangles and maybe some of the prison lice out of my hair. Pol packed his coffeepot into a bag, and Ambiades and Sophos put saddles on the horses.

The magus stood watching me. After a moment he opened his mouth to comment, and I expected him to suggest I cut the hair off, but instead he asked sharply, "Where did you get that comb?"

I looked at the comb in my hand as if perplexed. It was a nice one, probably very expensive. It was made from tortoiseshell, and it had long teeth and was inlaid with gold at the ends. "I think it's Ambiades's," I said at last. I'd taken it out of his pack.

Ambiades turned so quickly that the horse he was saddling

reared in alarm. He left it pulling at its head tie and crossed the clearing to snatch the comb out of my hand. He swung his fist toward my face, but this time I was ready, and he hit my shoulder as I turned away. Still, he knocked me backward off the stump where I was sitting and I landed in the dirt on the far side. I landed safely, but I yelped that my arm was broken.

For the second time that morning the magus was standing over me, this time looking concerned.

"Did you land on it?" he asked, bending down.

"No, the one he hit," I said. "He's broken my arm," which was a dreadful lie, and when the magus saw that, he stalked away in disgust.

He explained to Ambiades, loudly enough for everyone to hear, that if I'd fallen on my arm, I might very well have sprained a wrist and I would then be no use to him at all. "I thought I'd made that clear to you a moment ago." He punctuated his next few comments with blows to the head with that seal ring of his while I lay and listened to Ambiades yelp and resented being treated like a tool, even a valued one.

Once he had delivered his lecture, the magus left Ambiades to finish saddling up the horses, and went to repack the soap and his razor into his saddlebag. Several times I saw him look up with a puzzled expression, not at me but at Ambiades. If he thought he'd pounded good nature back into his apprentice, he was wrong. I saw the poisonous looks Ambiades sent back.

When Sophos was done saddling his horse and Pol's, he loaned me his own comb. I told him to his face that he was much too nice to be a duke. He blushed deep red and shrugged.

"I know," he said.

"So does his father," snarled Ambiades, leaning down from his horse as he rode by.

\*   \*   \*

It was not a propitious start to the day. Ambiades sulked for most of the morning, and Sophos rode with his shoulders hunched, trying to ignore the tension in the air. I reached up occasionally to check the size of my lip.

At one point I muttered, "You learn something new every day."

"What are you learning?" Sophos asked.

"To keep my mouth shut, I hope."

"You mean not bragging in wineshops that you're going to steal the king's seal ring?"

"That wasn't exactly what I was thinking," I said, "but you can bet I won't do that either. Tell me, if Ambiades has an exalted grandfather, why doesn't he have a better cloak?"

Sophos checked to be sure that Ambiades was riding ahead of the magus and out of earshot. "His grandfather was duke of Eumen."

I had to think for a minute. "Of the Eumen conspiracy?" I asked. I was quiet myself. Ordinary people didn't talk out loud about the Eumen conspiracy.

"After he tried to return the oligarchy and was executed, his family forfeited their lands and titles. I think Ambiades's father did inherit some money, but he lost most of it gambling. Last winter, when Ambiades wrote to his father and told him he needed a new cloak, his father sent him one of his old ones."

"Ah," I said. "Poor Ambiades."

Sophos looked at me sideways.

"How can he look down his aristocratic nose at the unwashed masses when he's as poor as anyone else, and landless to boot? I bet he wakes up every morning and can't stand it."

We stayed away from roads. Although we crossed many dirt tracks, we picked our way carefully between the trees and moved mostly at a slow pace. From time to time the magus checked the compass to make sure we stayed on course.

We stopped early in the evening as no moonlight would penetrate the crisscrossed leaves, but we were far enough from the nearest town that the magus approved a larger cooking fire, and Pol used some of the dried meat in the provisions to make a stew. There was no conversation around the fire as we ate. After dinner the silence was strained. Finally the magus spoke. "If Gen can take a few liberties with the old myths, I suppose I can, too," he said, and began to tell Sophos another story of the old gods.

# eugenides and the sky god's thunderbolts

After her argument with her consort, the Sky, Earth gave Hephestia her power to shake the ground. The Sky had promised to give Hephestia his thunderbolts, but he delayed. He made excuses. He'd sent them to be cleaned; he'd loaned them to a friend; he'd forgotten them by the stream when he was hunting. Finally Hephestia went to her mother and asked what she should do, and Earth sent for Eugenides.

Earth had promised that she would give no more gifts to him except those which she had given to all men. So she told Eugenides that he must use his own cleverness if he was to acquire the attributes of the gods. Cleverness was a gift she had given to all men, although to few had she given as much as to the woodcutter's son. She told Eugenides that the Sky sometimes lay in the evening with one of the goddesses of the mountain lakes, and when he did, he left his thunderbolts beside him.

Eugenides first went home to his mother and asked for the moleskin blanket that had covered him as a baby. He took the blanket to Olcthemenes, the tailor, and asked him to make a suit from it, both a tunic and leggings, and Olcthemenes, the tailor, did. Then Eugenides went into the forest and begged from every thrush a single feather, and he took those to Olmia, the weaver, and he asked her to make him a feathered hat and Olmia, the weaver, did. Then Eugenides climbed to the mountain lakes and he sat quietly in the cover of the trees and he waited for the Sky God to come.

When the Sky came to the lake in the late evening, he removed the thunderbolts from their shoulder harness, and he laid them down beside the lake. When all was quiet, Eugenides moved through the bushes, with hardly a sound, but the lake heard him. She said, "What was that that moved in the bushes?" And the Sky looked, and he saw the shoulder of Eugenides's tunic. He said, "Only a mole that sneaks through the twilight." And Eugenides moved still more quietly, but still the lake heard him, and she said, "What was that that moves through the bushes?" and the Sky looked, but not carefully, and he saw the edge of Eugenides's feathered hat, and he said, "Only the thrush that settles in the bushes to sleep." And Eugenides moved still more quietly and not the lake nor the Sky heard a sound as he slipped away with Sky's thunderbolts and carried them across the top of the mountain.

It was dark when the Sky went to retrieve his thunderbolts and when he could not find them he thought at first they were mislaid and he searched all over the mountaintops and it was day before he knew that they were gone.

He saw Eugenides crossing the plain at the base of the mountain, and he stopped him and demanded his thunderbolts. Eugenides said that he did not have them, and the Sky could see that this was true.

"Then tell me where they are," the Sky demanded, but Eugenides refused.

"I will take you in my hands and twist you back into dust," the Sky threatened, but Eugenides still refused. He knew that the Sky could not hurt him without breaking his promise to Earth. The Sky threatened and Eugenides was frightened, but he would not yield until the Sky agreed that he would give him whatever he asked if Eugenides would tell what he had done with the thunderbolts.

And Eugenides asked for a drink from the wellspring of immortality.

The Sky raged and Eugenides trembled, but he stood his ground, because bravery was a gift that Earth had given to all men and to her son in full measure.

Finally the Sky went to the wellspring and fetched a chalice of water, but he laced it with powdered coleus root before he gave it to Eugenides.

Eugenides told him where he had put the thunderbolts. "Look on my sister's throne in her hall where she will rule all lesser gods and you will see them." Then he drank the water and tasted the bitterness of the coleus root, and his mouth twisted.

"In the water of life," said the Sky, "the coleus will not harm you. But it has made the cup bitter as I will make your life bitter," and he left. He went to the Great Hall of the Gods to the throne of Hephestia to seek his thunderbolts, and he found them and Hephestia as well. The thunderbolts were resting in her lap. Hephestia made no mention of Eugenides. She only thanked her father for keeping his promise, and the Sky could not protest.

Thus the Sky made Eugenides immortal and yielded to

Hephestia the power of his thunderbolts. With those and the ability to shake the earth, she became the ruler of all gods except the first gods.

"Well done," I said when the magus finished.
"Why, thank you, Gen."
Did he sound genuinely flattered?

# chapter 7

*G*OOD FEELINGS PERSISTED between myself and the magus until the next morning, when Pol discovered that most of the food was missing from one of the packs of provisions. He called the magus over to him, and they talked quietly, throwing glances in my direction. The magus looked into the saddlebag himself and swore. He said something to Pol under his breath, and they both crossed the clearing to stand in front of me. The magus was carrying his horse crop in one hand. I stood up warily as they came.

"I hope you ate well?" said the magus.

"Not lately," I answered before I realized that another response might have been better.

"Hold him." The magus raised the crop. When Pol grabbed me by the arm, I ducked away, but I was too late. I planted my feet and tried to overbalance him but ended up with my head locked under his arm. I grabbed him around the knee and tried to throw him, but we both went down, and he landed on top. He shifted his weight until most of it lay on my head, and he held me pinned while the magus beat me across the back and shoulders with his horse crop.

I screamed curses—I am not sure what kind—into the grass and heaved with all my strength, but Pol would not be moved. He only ground my head harder into the dirt until I was exhausted and couldn't get my breath to yell anymore. The magus went on with a few strokes after that and stopped. When Pol released me, I grabbed his shirt in order to pull myself to my feet. He helped. As soon as I was up, I chopped him under the breastbone and left him gasping while I headed toward the magus. I had never been so angry in my life. Not even in the king's prison had I been this humiliated. If Pol had not grabbed me by the arm and jerked me backward, interposing himself, albeit hunched over and breathing painfully, between me and the magus, I am not sure what would have happened. The magus had taken one look at my face and was stepping back quickly.

I wasn't aware of any sound but Pol's labored breathing as the magus and I stared at each other. My mouth was so full of things I wanted to shout that I couldn't get any of them out. Which was just as well. If one thing had come, they all would have. How dare he treat me this way? How dare he? Finally I spat in his face. He jumped back further to avoid the spittle, and I turned away. I went to my blankets, where I threw myself down on my face and covered my head with my arms. I rubbed my face into the wool of the cloak rumpled underneath me, and except for that I didn't move all the time that Pol made breakfast and the others ate and packed up camp.

Pol came over and touched me lightly on the elbow. "Get up," he said very quietly. He didn't offer to help me, and I noticed when I did get up that he stayed out of arm's reach and watched me carefully, his weight forward on his toes.

Sophos was holding my horse. He'd moved it next to a stump that I could use as a mounting block, but I ignored the stump and pushed the horse away from it. Sophos came around the horse's head to offer me a leg up, but I ignored him as well. I put one foot into the stirrup and jumped onto the horse's back. I snapped the reins sharply to keep it from sidling, and the horse threw up its head in surprise.

I stopped to take a deep breath and let it out slowly. I could feel my eyebrows pressing together, and my teeth were so tightly clamped that the muscles in my jaw jumped. I took another breath and reminded myself that it wasn't the horse I was angry at. Nothing but my own ambition was keeping me near the magus. I could walk away from this party of overeducated adventurers if I chose. Neither the king's reward nor Pol could stop me, but I wanted to be a kingmaker myself. I wanted to be the first one to steal Hamiathes's Gift in hundreds and hundreds of years. I wanted to be famous. Only I couldn't steal the damned thing if I didn't know where it was, and only the magus could find it for me. I would stay with him until he led me to the stone, but I promised myself that someday I would stick a sharp knife into his arrogance and give it a good twist.

The magus and Pol had mounted their own horses.

"We'll swing west then to the stream and hope to find some kind of village somewhere along it? You think that's our best chance?" the magus asked Pol.

Pol nodded. The magus stuffed the map he carried in his hand into the bag behind his saddle. "This way then," he said, and led us through the trees. My horse followed just behind him as usual.

As we rode, I looked back over my anger from a little distance.

I'd been so mad that I'd frightened the magus, even with Pol between us. That was a new sort of event in my life, and I relished it a little as the morning passed. I was also pleased that I'd held my tongue. Saying things I shouldn't has been the origin of most of the painful episodes in my past, and it would certainly be an improvement in my character if I had a little more control over my own tongue.

"Are you okay?" Sophos whispered from beside me.

I looked at him from under my eyebrows, which were still drawn down. "Oh, sure," I said.

And I was okay. The horse crop hadn't been heavy enough to do any serious damage. The clothes the magus had supplied me with were thick enough to keep the skin from breaking. I wasn't disabled. My back hurt, but the fire would fade by nightfall, and whenever we got to wherever we were going, I would still be able to do my job. The magus would never do anything to impair my usefulness.

We came to a shallow river, bordered with scrub, and followed it upstream until we came to a break in the olive groves where other crops had been planted. The magus turned his horse and led us back into the trees.

"There will be a town somewhere close. Pol and I will ride in to get more food. Ambiades, I'm leaving you in charge. For gods' sakes, don't take your eyes off the thief." He didn't look at me as he spoke, but Ambiades cast a contemptuous glance in my direction.

I noticed that I had ceased to be "Gen" and returned to being a kind of unreliable animal, like a cow that's prone to wandering away. The magus and Pol left their horses and packs with us and set off up a trail that followed the river into town. What food there was they left in the backpacks and told us to eat for lunch. Sophos opened the bags and took out the bread and some warm sweaty pieces of cheese and handed them around. He gave me a loaf of bread to divide, and I kept most of it before passing the rest on to Ambiades. He protested.

"I didn't have any godsdamned breakfast!" I snarled, and he backed away. Evidently my anger was still effective. He wasn't going to bring up the reason I'd missed the morning meal.

After we had eaten the bread and the slippery cheese and were chewing on the dried pieces of jerky, Sophos said mournfully, "I'm still hungry."

I crossed my arms without saying anything. That was their tough luck.

"We could get some fish out of the river," Ambiades pointed out. "Pol has fishing line and hooks in his pack."

Sophos looked over at me.

"Don't expect my help," I said.

"We don't ever expect you to be helpful, Gen, but I'll bet you'll want some of the fish if we catch it," said Ambiades.

"I could fish and you could watch him," suggested Sophos. I saw that Sophos had also placed me in the category of unreliable livestock.

"You're terrible at fishing. You jerk the line and lose the bait."

"I could watch him while you fished."

Ambiades snorted. "If he got up and walked away, you wouldn't stop him. No. What we'll do is tie him up."

"You will not," I said.

"How?" Sophos ignored me.

"There's rope in the magus's pack. Go get it." Sophos went while I continued to protest.

"You're not tying me up. The magus said to keep an eye on me. He didn't say go fishing."

"Shut up," said Ambiades. "It's your fault there's nothing to eat."

"No," I said. "You're not going to tie me up."

I'd been sitting cross-legged on the ground. When Ambiades

leaned over me with the rope, I rolled away. He dropped on top of me, across my sore shoulders, and I yelped. He slipped a loop of rope over one of my hands and back, pulling the loop tight over the new pink skin on my wrist where the sores had almost healed.

"Don't." I yelped again. I grabbed the rope to keep it from pulling any tighter and tried to slip the loop off, but the rough rope dug into the tender skin. Ambiades yanked on the rope, pulling it out of my hand and tightening the loop.

"Hold still, or I'll pull it tighter," he said, and I gave up. I sat still while they tied my wrists and my ankles together, complaining the entire time.

"Be sure and make it tight," Ambiades told Sophos, who was working on my ankles.

"It's too tight," I said. "You're tying my hands too tight."

"Shut up," said Ambiades.

"Are you sure it's not too tight?" Sophos asked.

"Of course I'm sure. Have you got his feet done?"

"Ambiades"—I made one last effort to convince him—"you've tied my hands too tight. I can't feel my fingers. You have to loosen them."

"Maybe you should, Ambiades."

"Don't be stupid, Sophos, he's just saying that. Look, his hands are fine."

"They are not! Look." I held them up to Sophos. The pink skin on either side of the ropes was already puffy, but he was looking at my fingers.

"They aren't blue."

"They will be soon."

"They will not. Come on, Sophos." Ambiades had collected the fishing gear out of the magus's pack, and he pulled Sophos away.

I wanted to shout for them to come back, but I was afraid

that that close to an Attolian town, someone else might hear me. One curious villager could get us locked in a cellar until a queen's guardsman came to interrogate us. I didn't want to be publicly beheaded, and the ropes were not so tight that I couldn't stand them for a little while. I kept thinking that at any moment the magus or the Uselesses would be back. I sat and watched my hands turn blue.

Ambiades and Sophos didn't return from the river until they had seen Pol making his way down the riverbank. They found me lying on my side, breathing quietly and trying by mental effort to force the blood past the constricting knots and out of my hands, which were swollen and mottled.

"Oh, no," said Sophos.

"Damn right," I hissed, "get the ropes off. *Be careful!*" Ambiades had started tugging at the knots, and the pain was shocking. He jerked on the ropes and pulled the knots even tighter.

"Stop, stop," I said. "Just leave them. You can cut them off." But he wasn't listening. He managed to loosen one loop of rope, and he squeezed it over my fist, scraping the skin off my knuckles. "*You're killing me!*" I was reduced to yelling as Pol rushed into the clearing. He pulled Ambiades away and looked down at my hands and then at the fish lying in the dust, forgotten.

"Go get some more fish, both of you."

After a couple of uncertain steps backward, both Sophos and Ambiades turned and hurried into the bushes by the river. When they were gone, Pol set about carefully removing the knotted ropes. I didn't bother to whimper suggestively. I lay quietly while he cut the ropes away and only hissed when he pulled them away from the skin where they were stuck.

He started to straighten my curled fingers. "Don't," I said.

"They've got to be flexed. The blood has pooled."

"I'll do it," I promised, "myself."

After a moment he nodded.

"Where's the magus?" I asked.

"He sent me ahead with some of the food. It's a good thing." Pol looked over his shoulder to the river. "He doesn't need to know about this."

"Oh, yes, he does," I said. By that time I wanted to see Ambiades flayed alive.

"No," said Pol, "he doesn't." He crouched down a little more so that he could look into my eyes. "The magus has staked his reputation and his life to find this silly stone, wherever it is, and he'll murder the person who prevents him from getting it. And that person is not"—he shook his finger in front of my face—"going to be Sophos." I could see that there was no way to get Ambiades punished without dragging Sophos into trouble as well.

"His father sent me to make sure he's safe and that he learns something on this trip, but he is not going to learn what happens when you ruin the plans of a man like the magus." It was more words spoken altogether than I'd heard Pol use yet. He wrapped one hand in the fabric of my shirt and pulled my face closer to his. "My orders are to keep him safe and out of trouble. Whether we succeed in retrieving something from a fairy tale is not important to me. Do you understand?"

I nodded my head vigorously and then shook it back and forth. Yes, I understood, and no, the magus didn't need to be told after all. After all, when I thought about it, I had no grievance against Sophos, and Ambiades's hash I could settle on my own.

Pol went over to his pack to pull out the relief kit and brought back some bandages and salve to rub on my sore hands and a little paper packet of dried berries.

"Chew two of these," he said, "They'll help with the pain. We'll tell the magus that one of the sores reinfected."

"How long have I got, Pol?"

"Till what?"

"Till we get to where we are going."

"How would I know?"

"You know how much food the magus bought."

He thought for a moment. "Two more days."

The magus came back with the rest of the food and accepted Pol's story about my wrists without question. He only seemed concerned that the hands would be functional, and Pol reassured him. Ambiades looked scornful, but Sophos was visibly relieved. When we rode back into the olive groves, he moved his horse alongside mine and apologized very prettily. I told him to shut up and watched him blush. I don't know what had passed between him and Ambiades down at the river, but Ambiades seemed to have fallen quite off his pedestal. I thought he would probably climb back up again, but not soon. Meanwhile, Ambiades kept his horse near the magus, and Sophos fell back to ride beside Pol or sometimes beside me. I asked him why he had such a fancy cloak, and he blushed again. He was as regular as clockwork.

"My mother bought it for me when she heard I'd be traveling to the city to be with a new tutor."

"The magus?"

"Yes."

"Where were you before?"

"One of my father's villas. On the Eutoas River. It was nice there."

"But?"

"My father came for a visit and found out that I couldn't fence and I couldn't ride and I didn't like to go hunting. I liked to read instead." Sophos rolled his eyes. "He threw my riding instructor and my fencing instructor and my tutor out the front gate of the villa. Then he said Pol would teach me riding and fencing and I'd live with him in the city, where he could keep an eye on me."

"Pol is your father's man?" I glanced over my shoulder and met Pol's eyes for an instant before I turned back to Sophos.

"He's captain of my father's guard."

I whistled soundlessly. A man's son has to be pretty important to him if he has the captain of his own guard give him riding lessons and then does without his captain altogether so the son can have a bodyguard.

The olive groves changed in character as we moved through them. Instead of tightly packed rows of trees, there began to be space between the trunks. The irrigation ditches thickened with weeds and silt and were eventually choked out of existence. More dry oaks appeared, and we were eventually riding between trees that had gone entirely back to the wild.

"Doesn't anyone harvest these olives?" Sophos asked as he saw signs of old fruit rotted in the grass.

The magus overheard him. "Not anymore," he said over his shoulder. "Since the plague there aren't enough people in Attolia to harvest all these trees. The town where we bought provisions was probably once responsible for this part of the Sea of Olives, but there are only five or six families living there now, and they manage only the groves nearest them."

I knew about the plague years that had come thirty years before I was born. It had traveled with the trading ships across the middle sea, seeping through the lowlands and killing off entire families. In the wineshops in the city they said that as many as half the people in Sounis had died. All sea trade stopped. The crops rotted in the field, and Eddis had closed her passes, trying to keep the sickness out. My grandfather, who had been a young man during the plague years, had told me that no thief would touch the possessions of a plague victim for fear of contagion. Everything was burned.

"Are there places like this in Sounis," asked Sophos, "where there aren't enough people to farm the cultivated land?"

"Not many," the magus answered. "Sounis has always been a smaller country than Attolia, and so it already has a surplus population again. There are a few abandoned farms—the place we stayed before starting up the mountain, for example. The single surviving member of that family left the farm in order to go to the city to get an education."

"How do you know?" asked Sophos, always one to miss the obvious.

"I was he." The magus glanced over at me. Our horses, never moving swiftly between the trees, had stopped, and mine dropped its head to collect a snatch of tender grass. After a moment he said, "It's astonishing, Gen, but you are obviously thinking something, and I am curious to know what it is."

I was thinking of my numerous relatives, most of whom I had always considered a grievous burden, but if there hadn't been one that I loved, I wouldn't have landed myself in the king's prison. It was better, I supposed, to have all of them than none. I think it was the first generous thought I have ever had about some of my cousins. I told the magus, "I have an overabundance of relations, and I wonder if I am better off than you."

"You could be." He nudged his horse onward.

After a while Sophos started talking again. He was rarely quiet for long. "If there aren't enough people left in the village, why don't people move from somewhere else?"

"Where else?" the magus asked.

"The rest of Attolia?" Sophos hesitantly suggested.

"They're dead, too, stupid," Ambiades answered, and the magus winced.

"The plague thinned the population across the entire country," he explained more gently. "There are very few surplus people anywhere. Even in the cities."

"They could come from Sounis."

"Yes. They could." That was clearly what the king of Sounis had in mind.

"That would be an invasion," I said.

"So?" Ambiades challenged me.

"So the Attolians might object."

"But they aren't even using the land, Gen," Sophos protested. I wondered how he would feel if the positions were reversed and it was Attolia annexing the land of his people.

"They might object anyway," I said.

"That won't matter," said the magus.

"It will to the Attolians," I said to my horse.

At the end of that day we reached the edge of the Sea of Olives. We'd been following a wagon track, long overgrown. When it turned south, the magus led us away from it, back between the trees. A quarter of a mile further on the trees ended as if the gods had drawn a line across the earth from the cliffs on our left down to the river somewhere out of sight on our right. The mountains were black against the pink and blue evening sky. They'd been hidden by the trees for a long time, and it was reassuring to see them again.

Ahead of us there were no trees and few bushes of any kind. The earth was broken into ridges of rock and rubble. The setting sun threw black shadows across the black ground.

"What happened?" asked Sophos.

"It is the dystopia," said the magus. "We'll stop here for the night." He explained as Pol cooked dinner that the dystopia was the remains of the boiling rock that had poured out of the Sacred Mountain thousands of years before. The ground was rich with minerals, but it was too hard to allow plants to take root. It was difficult to cross and impossible to build a road through. It was as empty as any piece of land in the entire world.

"There is of course a myth to explain it," the magus said, yawning and rubbing his hands through his hair, "but I am too tired now even to listen to Gen tell it. So I will just say that Eugenides tried to use the thunderbolts he'd stolen from the Sky and started the fire that burned all this ground."

"He killed his brother," I said from where I was already lying on my blankets.

"Hmm? What was that, Gen?"

"His parents—not the Goddess, his mortal mother and father—had finally had children, and Eugenides killed his brother by accident in the fire. That's when Hamiathes saved him, and when Hephestia gave Hamiathes his gift to reward him because she was fond of her brother."

"So now we know everything," Ambiades said sourly from his blankets, and we all went to sleep without another word.

I had a strange dream that night of a marble-walled room and a woman in white, and I woke just as the moon was setting behind the olive trees. I had trouble getting back to sleep, so I sat up. Pol was on watch. If it had been the magus, he would have told me to lie down again. Sophos would have wanted to talk, but Pol just looked at me across the embers of the fire without a word. I stood up and paced a little back and forth, practicing my stretching exercises to loosen the muscles in my back. There were a few sore spots left from the magus's beating, but it was the pain in my wrists that bothered me. I cursed Ambiades under my breath and crossed over the fire to squat down near Pol.

"Those berries you gave me . . ."

"The ossil?"

"Do you have any more?"

He turned to his pack and pulled a small relief kit from it. Inside was a leather sack which held the berries. He poured out a small handful into his palm and then transferred them to my open hand.

"Only two at a time," he reminded me.

"Be blessed in your endeavors," I thanked him automatically, and popped the berries into my mouth before lying back down. I continued to flex my hands in training exercises until I was asleep.

The magus took fate in his hands the next morning and left Ambiades, Sophos, and me alone with one another again. He thought he had glimpsed a fire between the trees in the night, and he wanted to be sure we were unobserved when we crossed the dystopia. He and Pol went to scout. Before they left, Pol handed Ambiades and Sophos their wooden swords and told them to practice and do nothing else. Ambiades pretended not to understand, but Sophos nodded his head earnestly. They were both stretching out their muscles as Pol and the magus disappeared from sight.

As soon as they were gone, Ambiades turned to Sophos and poked him in the ribs with his sword. "Up and at 'em," he said.

"I haven't finished the stretching exercises," Sophos protested.

"Oh, forget them," said Ambiades. "You'll warm up as we go."

So Sophos put his sword into guard position, and they began circling each other. I watched them from where I lay with my head propped against a saddle. Ambiades struck over the top of Sophos's guard, but Sophos remembered his lesson and stepped to one side to block. He forgot, however, to follow through with a thrust after his block, and by the time he remembered, the opening in Ambiades's guard was closed.

"Good block," said Ambiades, trying to hide his surprise, and swung again. Sophos blocked, but he underestimated the force of the blow and had to back up to regain his balance. While he retreated, Ambiades pushed in and whacked him on the ribs. Sophos brought an elbow down to cover too late, as if an arm would have stopped anything but a wooden sword. Ambiades managed to whack it as he pulled his sword back. Sophos yelped, but Ambiades pretended not to hear, looking superior.

He rushed Sophos again and in the guise of fencing practice began to give him a series of bruises he wouldn't forget for a month. I was reduced to calling advice.

"Look," I said as they disengaged, "every time he tries to ride over the top of your guard, he leaves his right side open. Step left to block his attack and then counter immediately to his rib cage." I wasn't as patient as Pol. I couldn't wait for him to figure this out on his own.

"I'm sorry," said Sophos humbly. He was standing with his shoulders slumped, rubbing a sore elbow. He'd dropped his sword onto the dirt. "I'm just not fast enough. You're a better swordsman, Ambiades."

Ambiades shrugged as if to say, "Of course," and Sophos blushed. I snorted.

"All it shows," I said, "is that Ambiades is six inches taller than you and has a longer sword, as well as a longer sword arm."

The smug look gone, Ambiades turned on me. "What do you know about sword fighting, Gen?"

"I know your guard is terrible. I know that any opponent your size would cut you to pieces."

"Do you mean yourself?"

"I'm not your size."

"Coward."

"Not at all. If I got up and beat on you, Pol would come back and beat on me. I have work to do, and I don't like to work with bruises."

"Pol wouldn't know."

"Of course not."

Ambiades came to stand over me. "You're just a coward making excuses."

He kicked me in the side. It wasn't a heavy kick. But it was hard enough to leave a bruise in muscles that I might be needing at any moment.

"Ambiades, you can't." Sophos looked horrified.

"Do that again and I tell the magus," I said.

He leaned over me, his face ugly in contempt. "Gutter scum can't fight its own battles," he said.

"No," I said. "Gutter scum gets drafted into the infantry and fights for a worthless king, and hangers-on like you watch."

"Gen," Sophos protested, "that's treasonous."

"Do I care?" I said.

"Surprised, Sophos?" Ambiades's contempt made Sophos writhe. "His kind only ever serve themselves."

"Oh? And who else are *you* serving?" I asked him.

It had been a casual dig, but it hit a target. Ambiades's face twisted, and he swung his foot back, and that time he would have broken my ribs if I hadn't rolled away. When he lifted his foot to kick me again, I grabbed him by the heel and pulled him off-balance, then twisted in the dust to hook one foot behind his locked knee. He went down. I was almost to my feet and crouched to jump when the magus and Pol reappeared.

The magus raised his eyebrows. We separated. Ambiades got up and began brushing the dust off his sword. I lay back down with my head on the saddle.

"No unpleasantness, I trust?" said the magus. No one answered him.

After a very quiet discussion between the magus and Pol, we left the horses with Ambiades. The magus had wanted to leave

Sophos with the horses, but Pol wouldn't let him stay by himself and he wouldn't leave him with Ambiades either. It was clear that things had gone from bad to worse between Sophos and his idol.

So the magus, Pol, Sophos, and I headed into the dystopia on foot. I was more than glad to leave Ambiades behind. We walked all day, following the magus, who followed the directions of his compass. There was no trail at all, and we picked our way between and over the rumpled slabs of porous black rock. We carried our own water. There was none flowing in the dystopia, but there must have been some in the ground because grasses grew in clumps and bushes in larger clusters. Everything had dried to sticks and prickles that caught on our clothes as we passed. The rocks' rough surface tore cloth and rubbed raw skin that slid across it.

The magus explained to Sophos that more water moving across the lava could break it down into rich soil, but that this area was higher than the Sea of Olives and only had one river, the Aracthus.

"The Aracthus has carved itself a canyon and doesn't cause much erosion outside it. Later it reaches the plains below this and dumps what minerals it has collected there. That land is some of the best farming property in all Attolia."

"What about the Sea of Olives?" Sophos asked.

"It's a watershed for the winter rains that fall on the dystopia. Once the rains stop, most of the creeks empty and the land won't support crops. That's why it was all planted to olives before it was abandoned."

Crossing the dystopia, I again felt like a bug caught out in the open. My upbringing was making itself felt, and I longed to have more of the sky shut out. The mountains did rise in sheer cliffs on my left, but their steepness shut me out instead of enclosing me. I'd been more comfortable in the Sea of Olives.

In the evening we reached the Aracthus and turned upriver, toward the mountains. I tried to ignore the world stretching out forever behind my back. A few trees grew near the river, as well as bushes, and the lava flow didn't seem to be so much of a wasteland as it had. The river was narrow but deep in most places and had cut a channel as it twisted and banged against the rocky sides of its bed. Every once in a while it jumped over a shallow waterfall. Sometimes we walked along the edge of a chasm in which the water flowed; sometimes the chasm grew wider and shallower and we walked on the sand beside the river itself.

As the sun was setting, we hiked around a curve and came to a larger falls, maybe two or three times my height. The river was closed in on the side opposite us by bluffs. We could see the striations in the soil, all of them red or black. On our side the riverbank was almost flat, the lava had been ground into a beach, and behind us rose a more gradual hill that cut off the view of the dystopia between us and the Olive Sea.

The magus stopped. "This is it," he said.

"This is what?" I asked.

"This is where you earn your reputation."

I looked around at the empty rock and river and the sandy soil under my feet. As far as I could see, there was nothing to steal, nothing at all.

chapter 8

"WE'LL HAVE TO wait until nearly midnight," said the magus.
"We might as well get something to eat."

So Pol unpacked the backpacks and made dinner over a fire.
It took Sophos some time to find enough fuel to burn, but he
managed. I didn't help. I scuffed a hollow in the sand and lay
down in it to rest while I flexed my fingers in limbering exercises
and kneaded the wrists as much as I could stand to prevent
them from going stiff. I wondered what the magus thought we
were up to, out in the middle of nowhere, but I didn't ask. We
weren't on speaking terms. While Pol cooked, I napped.

The dream I'd had the night before returned. I was walking
up steps into a small room with marble walls. There were no
windows, but moonlight came from somewhere to fall on the
white hair and dress of a woman waiting there for me. She was
wearing the ancient peplos that fell in pleated folds to her feet,

like one of the women carved in stone beside old altars. As I entered the room, she nodded as if she'd been expecting me for some time, as if I were late. I had a feeling I should recognize her, but I didn't.

"Who brings you here?" she asked.

"I bring myself."

"Do you come to offer or to take?"

"To take," I whispered, my mouth dry.

"Take what you seek if you find it then, but be cautious. Do not offend the gods." She turned to the tall three-legged table beside her. It held an open scroll and she lifted a stylus and wrote, adding my name at the bottom of a long list and placing a small mark beside it. When I woke a moment later, Pol had dinner ready.

We ate by moonlight, without conversation, and then we sat. Nobody said much, and no one but the magus knew what we were waiting for. To break the silence, he at last condescended to ask me to tell him the story of Eugenides and the thunderbolts. He wanted to compare it with the version he knew.

I rubbed my arm across my forehead and yawned. I wasn't really in a storytelling mood, but neither did I want to sit in gloomy silence until midnight. I abbreviated the story a bit and told it to him.

## eugenides and the great fire

After Eugenides was born, the woodcutter and his wife had other children. The oldest of these children was Lyopidus. He was jealous of Eugenides because Eugenides had the gifts of the gods and because he was older. If the Earth had not given the woodcutter her own baby, Lyopidus would have been the first of his father's children, and he never forgot it. At dinner Eugenides sat on the right hand of their father, and when guests came to the house, it was Eugenides that offered them the wine cup.

When the the family's house was destroyed by the Sky God, Lyopidus was sure that Eugenides would be blamed. It was Eugenides who was the cause of the Sky's anger. Lyopidus wanted his father and mother to abandon Eugenides in the forest, but they would not. And when Eugenides stole the Sky God's thunderbolts and became immortal, Lyopidus's jealousy turned to hatred.

Eugenides knew his brother's feelings, and to avoid them, he traveled across the world. So Lyopidus sat at his father's right hand and offered his father's guests the wine cup, but he was still not happy. When the Sky God came to him in the guise of a charioteer with a plan to humiliate Eugenides, Lyopidus was ready to listen.

The Sky God took Lyopidus into his chariot and ferried him across the middle sea to the house where Eugenides lived, and Lyopidus went and knocked at Eugenides's door and said, "Here is a stranger who asks to share your wine cup."

And Eugenides came to his doorway, and he saw Lyopidus and said, "Brother, you are no stranger to me. Why do you ask to share my wine cup as a stranger when you are welcome to all I possess as my kin?"

"Eugenides," said Lyopidus, "in the past I had bad feelings for you, and now all those bad feelings are gone. That is why I say I am a stranger to you, and as an unfamiliar person I ask to share your wine cup and be your guest, so that you can discover if you like me and if you will call me friend as well as brother."

Eugenides believed him, so he fetched his wine cup and shared it with Lyopidus and called him his guest. But Lyopidus was no friend and no good guest. He asked his brother many questions, like how he hunted and how well he lived and what luxuries he had. Did he have a Samian mirror? An amber necklace? Gold armlets? An iron cooking pot? And each time Eugenides said no, he did not have that thing, Lyopidus said, "Why, I am surprised. You being a son of Earth."

And Eugenides said, "The Earth gives me no gifts that she does not give all men. I can hardly ask her to give every man an iron cooking pot in order to have one of my own."

"Ah," said Lyopidus, "then could you not steal one? As you stole the Sky's thunderbolts? But no," he said, setting out his hooks, "I suppose you could not do something so marvelous again."

"Oh, I could," said Eugenides, stepping like a mouse into a trap, "if I chose."

"Ah," said Lyopidus.

And every day Lyopidus tugged on the hooks he had set in Eugenides's flesh, begging him to perform some marvelous feat. "I could carry the word of it home to our parents," he explained. "They have not had news of you for so long."

For a time Eugenides evaded his request, but Lyopidus built up his arrogance, telling him over and over how clever he had been to defeat the Sky God, how much more clever he could be if he put his mind to it. For instance, he could steal the thunderbolts again, just for a lark, and then return them to Hephestia. He knew that Hephestia was fond of her half brother, part human and part god, and would not be angry at the trick.

After a time Eugenides agreed. He knew Hephestia would not mind, and he was eager to impress Lyopidus because he believed that Lyopidus wanted to be his friend as well as his brother. So he climbed one evening into a fir tree that grew in the great valley of the Hephestial Mountains and he waited for Hephestia to pass beneath him as she went to her temple at the summit. As she passed, Eugenides reached down and lifted the thunderbolts from her back, so lightly that she was unaware that they were gone.

He carried them to his house and showed them to Lyopidus, who pretended to be greatly impressed.

"You could throw one," he said. "If I tried to throw one, it would kill me, but you are part god."

"I suppose," said Eugenides.

"Try," said Lyopidus. "Just a small one."

And he nagged and cajoled, and to please him, Eugenides agreed to try. He chose one of the smaller thunderbolts, and he threw it against a tree, where it exploded and set the world on fire.

When the world began to burn, the Sky went to his daughter and said, "Where are the thunderbolts that I have loaned to you?"

"Here at my shoulder, Father," said Hephestia, but the thunderbolts were gone. Hephestia thought perhaps she had dropped them in the valley, so the Sky told her to go there and look and said that he would look with her.

"If you are so careless with them," he said, "I am not sure that I will return them to you if I find them."

From the valley Hephestia could not see the fire, and so the world went on burning. The olive trees burned and Eugenides's house burned. The fire grew, and Lyopidus was afraid. "You are immortal," he said to his brother, "but I will die." Eugenides took his hand, and they ran from the flames.

The fire surrounded them. Lyopidus cried out in his fear that it had been the Sky that drove him to entrap his brother, and he called on the Sky to protect him, but there was no answer. Eugenides loved his brother, as little as he deserved it, and he tried to carry him safely through the flames, but Lyopidus burned in his arms, while Hephestia and her father walked silently among the fir trees.

Now Hamiathes was king of one of the small mountain valleys. He looked down from his megaron and he saw the world burning and he saw Eugenides and his brother and he could guess the rest. He left his megaron and crossed the river to seek the great goddess in her temple, but her temple was empty. He turned back to the river and met at its bank the river god who was a child of the Sky.

"The world has caught fire," he told the river.

"I will not burn," said the river. "I am water."

"Even water is injured by a great fire," said Hamiathes, thinking of the burning when the Sky and the Earth were angry with each other.

"Where is the fire?"

"Below us on the plains."

"Above my course or below it?"

"Below."

"Then I do not need to worry," said the river.

"But Eugenides will suffer."

"Eugenides is the enemy of my father," said the river, and Hamiathes saw that he would get no offer of help from the river, so he stood for a moment in silence and watched the world burn, and Lyopidus die, and Eugenides burned and did not die.

"Look," he said to the river, "Eugenides carries the thunderbolts of your father."

"They are no longer my father's," said the sullen river. "Let Hephestia fetch them herself."

"If you fetched them, you could give them to your father and not to Hephestia," Hamiathes pointed out.

"Ah," said the river, and after a moment asked, "Tell me where to change my course that I may fetch the thunderbolts."

And Hamiathes told him. "If at this point you leave your course and go with all your strength, you will flow across the plain to Eugenides."

The river did as Hamiathes instructed, and as he flowed across the plain, he cut through the heart of the fire and quenched it, and as he reached Eugenides, his power was almost spent. He swept up the half god along with the thunderbolts because Eugenides would not release them, and the river's new course carried them both down to the great river, the Seperchia, who was the daughter of the Earth.

She said to the lesser river, "You are tired. Give me the thunderbolts that I may return them to my sister."

While the smaller river and Seperchia fought for possession of the thunderbolts, Hamiathes went to the temple of the great goddess Hephestia to await her return. And Eugenides, ignored by the two rivers, swam to the bank and pulled himself out of the water, burnt as black as toast. And that is why Eugenides, alone among the gods, is dark-skinned like the Nimbians on the far side of the middle sea.

It was not my favorite story, and I wished I hadn't brought it to mind just then, when I had work to do.

"Did you know," I asked the magus, "that when you think someone is very intelligent, you say he is clever enough to steal Hamiathes's Gift?"

The magus cocked his head. "No, I didn't. Is it just among your mother's people?"

I shrugged. "I don't know. But I know what happened if you tried and got caught."

"I don't know that either," the magus said, surprised by a gap in his scholarship. He wasn't surprised that I knew. I suppose crime and punishment are things that most thieves keep track of.

"They threw you off the mountain."

"Maybe that's what happened to your mother. Maybe that's why she left Eddis." He was teasing, doing his best to lift my spirits. He'd either gotten over his anger or was pretending that he had.

"Not threw as in exile," I said, and described with one hand the arc of someone falling a long distance. "Threw as in *over the edge of the mountain.*"

"Oh," he said.

We were all quiet again. It was another quarter of an hour before we heard the sound the magus had been waiting for. It was a variation in the wash of the river beside us. The magus stood and turned to look at it. I did the same, and in the space of a few heartbeats the river disappeared. The flow of its water stopped, came again in slushy bursts over the falls, and then stopped again. It was as if a giant tap somewhere had been turned by the gods, and our ears, which had ceased to register the sound of water, were now pounded by the silence of no water at all.

I stood with my mouth open for a long time as I realized that upstream there was a reservoir and the water that made the Aracthus flowed through a sluice in its dam. At the end of the summer, if the water in the reservoir was too low, then the sluice gate was closed and the river disappeared. I shook my head in wonder.

In the bulging rock where the waterfall had been, there was a recessed doorway. The lintel of the doorway was the rock itself, but set into it were two granite pillars. Between the pillars was a door pierced by narrow slits that were wider in their middles and narrower at the ends. The river water still sprayed through these slits and dropped into the round pool that remained in the basin below.

"I wanted to get here at least a day early, to give you a chance to rest," said the magus. "The water will begin to flow again just before dawn. You have to be out again before that, as I believe the temple will fill quickly. I assume that you will need these." He handed me the tools of my trade, wrapped in a soft piece of leather.

I recognized them. "These are mine."

"Yes, they were the ones taken from you when you were arrested. Not being a thief, I couldn't otherwise be sure of equipping you properly."

My stomach was jumping as it hadn't since the audience with the king. "You already knew then?" I asked.

"Oh, yes, the man you bragged to in the wineshop was an agent of mine. Not just a casual informer."

I whistled soundlessly as I thought of the twists in this tale. "I need a light," I said.

"Pol has one for you."

I looked behind me and saw Pol standing with a lamp in his hand. He gave it to me. "There's six hours of oil."

"Do you have a pry bar?" I asked. It was the only necessity that I didn't habitually carry with the rest of my tools because it was too big. Pol did have one and went back to his pack to fetch it. I walked to the edge of the riverbank. The water left in the pool still rippled against it.

"If my calculations are correct, the water will stop for four nights in a row this year, and this is the second of them. Don't get yourself drowned on the first try," said the magus.

Pol handed me the pry bar, and it was a comfort to have it in my hand, even though I could be sure that there was nothing living in the temple. You can't keep watchdogs someplace that's underwater all but a few nights of the year. Snakes, though, I thought. Maybe you could keep snakes.

I waited another half an hour until the water flowing through the slits in the doorway had lessened its force. Then I stepped into the pool. Standing up to my ankles in water, I turned back to ask the magus, "Do you know if anyone has tried this before?"

"I believe that several attempts have been made," he said.

"And?"

"No one came back."

"From inside?"

"No one who has been inside has returned; no member of any party where someone went inside has returned either. I don't know how it might happen, but if you fail, we are all lost together." He smiled and waved one hand in a vague benediction.

I nodded my head and turned back toward the doorway. I wondered when I reached it how old it was. I ran my hand up and down the smooth granite of a pillar. There were gentle undulations where the stone had once been fluted. The door hanging between the pillars was stone as well. Wood would have rotted, and metal would have worn away. I poked my finger into one of the slits, widened by years of flowing water. It looked thin in relation to the size of the door, but it was wider than my hand, even at its narrow end.

The door was three or four feet above the level of the pool, and I scrambled onto its threshold, careful not to spill the oil in the lamp. Even the hinges of the door were made from stone, and it was difficult to shift, but there was no lock on it. I pushed against not only its weight but the weight of the water remaining behind it. As I pushed, I muttered a perfunctory prayer to the god of thieves. It was a superstition my grandfather had ingrained in me. Send up a prayer as you start your work, send up a prayer as you finish it, and leave a gift once a month on the altar of Eugenides. I liked to leave earrings myself. My grandfather had left fibula pins.

The door swung inward, and more water rushed out. Once I was through, the water swung the door closed behind me. I was wet to my waist, but the water on the stairs behind the door was only three or four inches deep. Still, it flowed quickly, and I had to place my feet carefully as I climbed up the steep steps to the room above, where I recognized the chamber I'd seen in my dreams.

The smooth marble walls were marked with river silt, and the floor was deep in water that flowed through the grille in a door opposite me. The moonlight I'd dreamt of fell through an irregular hole in the ceiling, but there was no woman in a white peplos waiting for me. No gilded table, no scroll.

I stood under the hole in the ceiling and looked up. When the river came back, it would pour first into the chamber, backing up to fill the temple. When the room and the temple were full, some water would still flow through the chamber, but most would carry over the top to the falls and hide the doorway in the rock face. It was a work of genius, and I wondered how long ago it had been built. Five hundred years, if it had been meant to hold Hamiathes's Gift.

I crossed the room to the doorway on the far side. As I did so, I remembered the questions of the woman in white. If I had been a religious person, I might have stopped to pray in earnest, but it didn't occur to me.

Like the outer door, the inner door was stone, but its lower half was a barred grate to admit water more easily. It had no lock, just a simple latch, a stone locking bar fitted into a bracket. The open bars of the grate allowed the latch to be lifted from either side. I stopped to light my lamp, then pulled open the door. It, too, swung closed behind me.

The corridor on the other side stretched in two directions and was so narrow that my shoulders brushed its walls. They were solid rock. Lumpy and wet, they sagged inward near the roof to form an arch, with an apex lost beyond the feeble light of my lamp. In each direction the corridor ran for about ten feet, then turned and ended in a locked door. Here, where the flow of water was less strong, the doors were metal with metal locks. There was no sign of rust.

The locks were complicated, and it took me several minutes to get the door on the right open. Beyond it was another stretch of narrow corridor, which again ended with a door similar to the one I held open. I sighed, and hunted around for something besides my foot to jam under the door. I didn't want to have to reopen it in order to let myself out.

There were no loose stones in the tunnel. There was the leather bag I used to hold my tools or the pry bar. I certainly didn't want to let go of the pry bar. In the end I used one of my shoes. They were soaking wet anyway and uncomfortably heavy. I took them both off and tucked one into my belt, in case I needed it later. The other I wedged under the door so that it wouldn't swing shut and relock behind me. Barefoot, I stepped carefully down the corridor through several inches of water, which were still draining from the temple. I was only halfway to the far door when the lamplight revealed something noteworthy about its surface. It was perfectly smooth. If there was a lock on the door, there was no keyhole on this side to open it.

"Gods," I said aloud, "oh, gods," and turned back to the door behind me as the water washed my shoe out from beneath it and it began to swing closed.

I leapt—four giant steps—and threw myself face forward toward the closing door and slipped my fingers ahead of it into the jamb. The metal door bit into my fingers, but I left them pinned until I could slip my other hand into the precious opening they had preserved. This door, like the other, was perfectly smooth on the inside.

I scootched through the doorway on my bottom and sat in the outer hall sucking my injured fingers. I still had my tools, but I had dropped the pry bar and the lamp. The only light I had came from the moon by way of the grille in the stone door behind me. It was not much.

When my heart stopped pounding and the pain in my fingers lessened, I stood up and paced. There was no point in opening the doors without a better means of holding them open, but I didn't want to waste the time it would take to go back out to the magus to get another lamp and a pry bar and door blocks. Really, I didn't want to tell him that I'd nearly gotten myself irretrievably stuck before I even reached the interior of the temple. Not that I would have died immediately if I had been trapped. I wouldn't have died until morning, when the river returned. Just thinking about it made my heart pound again. I was a thief, I had to remind myself, of some accomplishment, or I would have been caught. I decided to check the other door before I went out to find door blocks.

I didn't need a light to work by, but there was a dent across the ends of the first two fingers on my right hand, and their tips were numb. That made it difficult to open the lock on the second door. Once I had it open, I checked for a keyhole in its far side. I even checked to be sure that the keyhole I felt with my fingertips was a real one, not a blind hole drilled there to deceive me. Once I was sure that I would be admitted to the workings of the lock, I wedged the door open with my remaining shoe—the other was lost—and crossed the threshold. It was pitch-dark ahead of me. Without the oil lamp I couldn't see if this tunnel was a twin to the first one.

I dug my hands into the pockets of the blue trousers the magus had given me. One pocket had filled with water and was soaking wet; the other had remained fairly dry. I had matches in both. I'd picked up a package of sulfur matches in a little silver case at the inn the first night on the road, and I'd picked up another five or six the second night. The ones I'd taken from Pol were wrapped in a scrap of oiled paper. The water wouldn't have bothered them. In the dry pocket I also had a small knife with a folding blade that had belonged to the man sitting next to us at lunch one day, several pieces of leather thong, one longer piece of cotton twine, and the fibula pin that the magus used to hook his cloak. He thought he'd dropped it before his last bath, stupid man. In the wet pocket were miscellaneous coins, two moist pieces of jerked beef, and Ambiades's comb. I wondered if he'd noticed yet that it was missing.

I put one of the pieces of beef in my mouth and chewed it while I thought. I could always turn back to fetch door blocks and another light, but I didn't really need them. I had no doubts about my ability to open any locked door, so long as it had a keyhole, and I was used to working with no light. I dug out a match from the silver case and lit it. There before me was the corridor mined out of the solid rock, with another metal door at the end. Leaving my shoe to wedge the door as well as it could, I went forward. The match burned down to my fingers; I blew it out and continued in the dark.

The door was locked. I opened it and had to let it close behind me, but I checked the keyhole on the far side first. Beyond the door was another corridor, no different. I lit a match and then felt my way along the stone walls in the dark. The floor was uneven, and I stubbed a toe once but placed my feet more carefully after. I didn't hurry. As my hands brushed across the stone on one side of me, they touched something cold and hard and perfectly smooth. I stopped and felt more carefully and then lit a match to see what I had found. It was Hephestial glass, obsidian, formed when the rock I walked through had been heated to liquid and had flowed across this part of the world. In ancient times it had been mined and used for points on arrows and spears, and it was still treasured for jewelry and the blades of decorative knives. The piece in front of me was the size of my head and would have been very valuable if I'd had some way to pry it out of the wall.

I walked on, and my sliding fingers touched another piece and another. I lit a match and found myself at an intersection of corridors. I walked in corridors all night—a maze of corridors hollowed out of the stone bluff. I wandered through it perplexed.

At one point I was surprised to find myself back at the door where I had come in. I hadn't expected it to appear at the end of a corridor, and I stopped to think. Trying to arrange a map in my head of someplace I'd traveled through in the dark was difficult, but I'd had practice. I should not have arrived back at the door where I had come in, I was sure. I lit another match and checked the keyhole; then I forced the lock with my tools. I opened the door and felt along its opposite side and found no opening. This was not the door I had come in, although it was identical. Even the irregular shape of the stone walls leading to it looked the same. This was the other end of the trap. I lit yet another match—I had only seven left—and there on the floor ahead of me was the pry bar and beyond it, tipped on its side, the little brass lamp.

Of course, I thought. I will just step through this door and fetch my pry bar and my lamp and the door will close behind me and I will be trapped forever. Not likely. But I did want the lamp, so I held the door open with my foot—it was heavy and pinched the skin—while I pulled my overshirt over my head and wedged it very firmly beneath the door. Then I pulled off my undershirt as well and left it in a pile to block the doorjamb, just in case. Then, half naked and shivering, I hurried into the trap, picked up my lost possessions (no sign of my shoe), and hurried out again. Safe.

Some of the oil had spilled out of the lamp, but there was plenty left. I lit it and wandered through the corridors I had seen only with my fingertips. It wasn't a big maze, not really big enough to get lost in. I thought of the temple to the goddess of the spring where we had stopped on the mountainside. It had been a small temple for a minor deity, and this maze was not much bigger than that temple, maybe two times its size, maybe three. And there didn't seem to be a temple, at least no temple like any that I had ever seen. There was no naos, so of course no pronaos, no altar, no statues of the gods or of their supplicants. Most important there was no opisthodomos, no treasure room to store valuable offerings. Instead there was this maze of corridors hollowed out of the stone bluff.

The magus had been swoggled, I would have thought, except for one thing. At the back of the maze, farthest from the entrance doors, was a wider corridor, more carefully finished than the others. Its floor was canted, and one side was the lowest point in the maze. The water that remained there was several inches deep, but not deep enough to cover the bones that had settled over the years and remained undisturbed as the Aracthus drained away.

There were skulls worn as thin as eggshells, longer bones like thighbones, and smaller curved ribs that poked one end out of the dark water. How long, I wondered, does it take bones to dissolve? Fifty years? A hundred years? How long had these bones been here and how many had disappeared before them? I trailed my fingers in the water and shuddered at the cold. How could so many people have come searching without leaving a record? How could Hamiathes's Gift have remained lost if so many people had known to look for it here? The light of my lamp reflected off the water, hiding some of the bones and revealing others, small bones, still arranged in the shape of a hand. I stepped back and left the surface of the water dark. I went back to check each corridor again for an opening that I might have missed.

There was none, but passing with my lamp where I had been only in the dark, I realized the abundance of the Hephestial glass. There were veins of it that sloped diagonally past me, three inches wide and twelve feet long. There were lumps of it two feet across, even three feet. They were perfectly black and at the same time filled with the different colors of my lamplight. They were so much like windows into the stone walls that I laid my hand against the glass to block reflections and I tried to look through them, as if I could see into the walls beyond.

In the longest corridor in the maze, excepting the one with the water and the bones, there was an enormous piece of obsidian, veined with solid rock. It started a little above the floor and reached over my head in a bulging sort of trapezoid. I ran my hands over it and thought of the hundreds of pendants, earrings, brooches, and spearpoints it would make.

I was standing there before it when the panic came. The walls pressed in, and the water seeped through them. The flame in my lamp sputtered, and I remembered the passage of time. Pol had said there was six hours of oil . . . but I had wandered for a long time by matchlight . . . but some of the oil had spilled from the lamp when I dropped it. How much time did I have? How much oil? I sloshed the lamp from side to side as my feet began moving of their own volition toward the door of the maze. I was careful to turn in the direction of the true exit. A careless thief or a panicked one might mistake the one door for the other and not realize his error until he was trapped, but I would not be careless.

The panic grew stronger. At the first locked door I spilled my tools out of their leather wrapper. The false keys, the awl, the tumbler jams—everything scattered on the stone floor, and I had to kneel down to gather them up. My hands shook. I nearly dropped everything again before I worked the lock open and stepped through the door into a puddle that hadn't been left by the receding river. It was the first sign of the Aracthus's return.

Panting with haste, I rushed to the next door and forgot my lamp behind me. I went back for the lamp, then turned again to the exit. It had swung closed sometime during the night, pushing my shoe ahead of it. Water poured through the grille in its bottom, washing toward me. Frantically I worked the lock. As it released, the door leapt open—I narrowly avoided being hit in the face—and the water behind it surged in, pushing me backward. I swung my arms for balance, dropped the pry bar, and let it go. I waded upstream to the barred stone door between me and the antechamber to the maze where the water came in through the ceiling. Waves sloshed in the tiny room.

I lifted the locking bar on the door and opened it, then edged my way along the wall of the antechamber and down the stairs. The water was still only five or six inches deep, but it had backed up against the door at the bottom where its path was restricted to the narrow slits in the door. With the strength that comes from terror I pulled the door open, against the force of the water; then the water and I both rushed out over the threshold. The door slammed behind me with force enough to break bones.

I landed on my hands and knees in the pool below and got up soaked and spluttering. I'd been wet all night, and I felt like a fool. The panic was gone. The maze behind me wouldn't be full for hours yet. I could hardly have drowned in six inches of water.

As I waded toward shore, it was easy to imagine how undignified my arrival in the pool must have looked from the riverbank. There was no sun in the sky, but the world was twilight gray. In an hour it would be dawn.

"Did you get it?" the magus asked from the bank.

"No." I sloshed toward him sullen and embarrassed. "I couldn't find it. I couldn't find anything." Nothing except huge chunks of obsidian. "There's no naos, no altar, no treasure room." I told him about the maze as I climbed up the sandbank out of the water. "It's not very big." He reached out a hand to help, grabbing me first above the wrist and then behind the elbow.

"There're still two nights left," he said optimistically. "Come get some breakfast."

We woke Pol, who made us breakfast. He'd been hiding six eggs in his bags as well as more coffee. The magus dug out a dry set of clothes for me, and after breakfast I lay down and went to sleep. The sun was just rising.

chapter 9

_I_ SLEPT THROUGH the day with sunlight and blue sky filtering through my closed eyelids. After a cold, wet night in the temple maze, the sun was contentment itself, and I didn't wake until it was setting. I had been dreaming again of the lady in the chamber; her hair was held away from her face by a string of dark red stones set in gold. She used a swan feather pen to put a second mark by my name, and she seemed concerned for my sake. I was about to ask where was the temple, where was the altar and the statue of the goddess, when the smell of coffee woke me.

I groaned as I woke. My eyes were still closed as I stretched my muscles, my arms over my head. There was someone standing above me, Sophos, I thought. He put a little cup of coffee in my outstretched hand.

"Gods bless you," I said to him.

"You're welcome," said the magus dryly. "When you have returned to the land of the living, I have some questions to ask."

I scowled and took my time over the coffee. It was thick and sweet, and I was sorry when I reached the grounds at the bottom of the cup.

The magus had many questions. First, though, he asked me to describe my night in the temple. I told him about the corridors mined out of the solid rock with their walls sagging in to make arched ceilings. I told him about the trap and how I'd almost been caught in it. I didn't tell him about the antechamber that I recognized in my dreams. I didn't really believe that myself, and only reluctantly did I tell him about the pool of bones.

"How many bones?" he wanted to know.

Ghoul, I thought. "The skulls were in pieces, I saw parts of four or five, maybe more. Does it matter?"

"My predecessor came here, I think," the magus explained. "But as far as I know, he came alone. The other bones would be older. I wish I knew . . . " he murmured.

"Knew what?"

"Knew why whole expeditions have disappeared after this goal."

"I wish I knew," I said, "how the bones came to be piled in the back of the maze and none of them left in the trap at the front."

The magus raised his head to look at me and then raised his eyebrows as well. "An astute observation," he said. "Somebody moved them?"

I shrugged. I didn't know. Maybe in five hundred years every thief that came here had been as smart as myself, but I found that difficult to believe. I looked around the campsite as a different thought occurred to me.

"I'd move camp if I were you," I said.

"Why?"

"The river turns here. We're right across from the falls. If the water came back faster than it did last night, it would jump that falls and land on top of you. You and Pol and Sophos would be washed across the sandbar and end up somewhere downriver, probably drowned."

The magus nodded. "We'll move. Eat some dinner."

While I ate, I asked Pol if he had any rope or twine. I needed a piece longer than the ones I'd had in my pockets. After dinner I changed back into my clothes of the night before. Everything but one pocket lining had dried in the sun while I slept. Just after midnight the river sloshed in its bed and disappeared. It was as magical the second time as it was the first. I waited longer for more of the water to be gone from the maze before I took the line that Pol offered me and stepped into the pool.

I slipped through the stone door in the bluff and found one of my shoes. It was bobbing in the little bit of water still trapped behind the door. The other shoe had been dropped by the receding water in a corner of the antechamber. I put them on and grimaced with distaste. They were cold. I lifted the locking bar on the inner door and stepped into the maze. By the time I had opened the locks on the metal door my body heat had warmed the shoes on my feet and I had forgotten them.

Locks are not difficult things to open. They all work on the same system: Little tumblers keep the lock closed in this position and open in that position. The more tumblers you have, the more expensive the lock, but if a thief can open a lock with four tumblers, he can open one with six or eight or twelve almost as easily. He just uses a longer false key with adjustable strikes to move the tumblers.

If you want to keep something safe, I say hire a guard, at least until someone invents a better lock. Or hide your treasure where no one will find it. That's what most people do. Being able to find valuables in boxes hidden behind bed frames, being able to move through a building with no one the wiser, those are more important skills for a thief than opening locks. Those and a good head for heights. People don't usually hide their emerald earrings in the cellar.

I blocked open both of the metal doors with stones I'd brought from the riverbank and wandered through the maze to the pool of bones. I stood and looked at it for a while with the light of my lamp reflecting off the dark water. This was the one place in the maze that might hold Hamiathes's Gift, and I didn't want to look. I paced the length of the pool a few times before I started at one end and raked my fingers through the cold water, disturbing silt and bones. I found a ring, two rings, gold buttons, silver buttons, brass buttons, fibulas, brooches. The thieves who had come to this place had been a wealthy bunch, but none of them had found what they came for. The brooches were set with lapis and obsidian and a variety of other stones, but none of them was Hamiathes's Gift. There was one ring that held a large green emerald engraved with a design I couldn't make out in the dim light. It was too big for my finger. I slipped it over my thumb. The rest of the things I'd found I shoveled back into the pool, offerings to the gods.

I left that corridor and began the tedious work of measuring the maze, using the line Pol had given me. It took all night. I was just finishing when the panic came again. I coiled the rope with shaking hands and hurried toward the exit of the maze. By the time I reached the doors I was running and I almost collided with the first one. It was closed. My stone block had not stayed in position even though I had placed it carefully and wedged it firmly so that it would hold against the returning Aracthus. I fumbled for my tools and unlocked the door. When I started for the next one, which I could see was also closed, my foot kicked the stone door block, lying where it had been pushed by the swinging door. My other foot kicked the pry bar which I had dropped and forgotten the previous night. That was a more painful impact, but I didn't stop. I limped on as quickly as I could to the tar door and through it and out of the maze. My exit was perhaps a little more dignified than the night before, but not much. The magus was waiting for me.

"Any luck?" he asked.

"None," I said.

"Dammit. What are you doing all night?"

"Tripping over pry bars," I told him. "Where's my breakfast?"

After I ate, I asked the magus if he had any paper. I knew he had a journal that he kept a record of our days in.

"Did you want to write a letter to your sweetheart?" he asked.

"What makes you think my sweetheart can read? Shut up and get me a piece of paper."

The magus laughed and pulled himself up to walk to his backpack, lying beside his bedroll. He tore a sheet from the back of his journal and flourished it in front of me. "I hear and obey," he said, "which is more than you have ever done."

I snatched the paper out of his hands and noticed Sophos staring in astonishment. "What are you looking at?" I asked him.

"Nothing," he answered.

"He is merely astounded by my good humor, Gen," explained the magus, "and my ready compliance to your grumpy requests." To Sophos he said, "I have the highest respect for a craftsman, and Gen is nothing if not that. Although if he doesn't bring back Hamiathes's Gift tonight, the three of us may as well drown here as go back and tell the king that we have failed."

"The three of you?" I asked pointedly. "What happens to me?"

"Oh," said the magus, waving one hand, "you would drown in the maze."

A chill shivered down my spine. I turned to the paper in my hand without speaking. I used a charcoal stick from the fireside to mark out the measurements I'd stored in my head. The maze took shape under my hands while the magus looked silently over my shoulder.

"What's that?" He pointed with a finger at a dark smudge.

"A mistake," I answered. "I keep getting my measurements turned around. That big piece of obsidian that I told you about, though, is right there." I marked it with another smudge.

"If I were here to get rich, I'd be a happy man. How long is the rope?" he asked after a pause.

"About thirty feet," I told him.

"Thirty exactly," Pol volunteered.

"So this space here"—the magus put his fingertip down on the page—"might be as much as eight feet by six?"

"I think so," I told him.

"You think there is a room hidden?"

"I don't know. Every wall is two feet or three feet thick. There could be a hidden storage space anywhere. And then there are the outside walls of the maze. A secret way could lead to a tunnel a mile long. I just don't know."

"You've checked those walls?"

"Every inch," I said, frustrated.

The magus squeezed one shoulder. "If there were a door, you would find it, Gen," he said, and I shrugged. I was pessimistic of finding anything hidden in any of the seamed walls of the maze. There was no door. I was positive of it.

"Did you look among the bones?" he asked quietly. He hadn't suggested it the night before, although the necessity was obvious to both of us.

"Yes."

"Find anything?"

I looked down at the ring still hung around my left thumb. He looked as well and whistled. In the sunlight I could see that the emerald was flawed, milky white on one side. The seal engraved in it was a curving fish, maybe a dolphin. The white flaw was a breaking wave.

The magus leaned over me to lift it off my thumb. "The writing on the ring itself is in the old style, pre-invader. Whoever wore it here must have had it in his family for many generations."

"Or he lost it here a long, long time ago."

The magus agreed. "Or that. I'll put it in my bag, so that it doesn't get lost."

"You will not," I said. The ring didn't belong in a bag; it belonged on a finger. My finger.

The magus looked down at me, and I started to get up. Pol rose as well.

"If you want a seal ring," I said, louder than I'd intended, "go get one yourself."

"Oh, very well." The magus capitulated with a smile, handing it back to me. "Grave robber."

I laughed at that. "I'm trying to rob a god's temple, and you think I should worry about the ghosts of a few dead men?" I slipped the ring back over my thumb and went to lie down. With the image of the maze in my head, I slept.

And dreamed again. In the antechamber the woman in white called me by name. Of course she had written my name on her scroll, I knew that, yet hearing her say it aloud tore away a comforting pretense of anonymity. I hesitated, and she called me again.

"I am here," I answered.

"Many have sought twice in the maze and yet gone away," she said quietly. "If you go a third time into the maze, you will not leave without what you seek."

I nodded my head.

"You will go a third time?"

"Yes."

"There is no shame if you did not." She paused as if she had wandered as far as she could from a script that was written out for her. "Who brings you here?" she asked.

"I bring myself," I whispered.

"Then will you go?"

"Yes."

"Be cautious," she said as she turned and picked up her white pen. "Do not offend the gods."

I woke before she looked up from the third mark beside my name.

It was still more than an hour before sunset. The sand under me was warm with a day's heat, and I was comfortable. I stayed where I was with my eyes closed and thought about the stones I'd used as door blocks the night before. They shouldn't have moved. I had been very careful. Had someone removed them? A woman in white? A little voice inside me laughed. Of course she knew my name. She was a dream, something made of my own imagination. If I knew my name, then so did she, but those blocks hadn't been moved by a dream.

I opened my eyes in slits and looked over at the magus. He and Pol were sitting by the cold fire ring talking quietly, so as not to wake me, about some army campaign they had fought together. Pol wouldn't have moved the blocks. He didn't particularly care if I found the stone, but he was no enemy to the magus. The magus could have moved the blocks, but I couldn't see why he would. I had an ugly image of him sealing the outer door of the maze and refusing to let me out until I produced Hamiathes's Gift, but it was a nightmare, nothing real. The magus, in spite of his dogged pursuit of world sovereignty for Sounis, was a reasonably honest man. When I'd accused him of intending to knife me in the back after I'd delivered Hamiathes's Gift, he'd been insulted and angry. He'd steal an entire country, but he wouldn't murder one dirty little thief. Nor would Pol, unless the magus ordered it, nor did I need to worry about

Sophos as an assassin. Ambiades I would worry about, but we'd left him on the far side of the dystopia.

So who had moved the blocks? No one, I finally decided. The doors were heavier than I'd allowed for, the wet stone slicker. I'd have to be more careful, that was all. My stomach rumbled for the lunch it had missed, and I sat up.

"Welcome," said the magus. "Would you like some dried beef, some dried beef, or some dried beef for lunch?"

"Oh, I'll take stuffed pigeons in sauce, thank you, and some decent wine to drink. None of that cheap stuff, please."

The magus handed me an almost empty paper package of dried beef and half of a loaf of bread. "Enjoy your meal," he said.

The bread was four days old and as difficult to chew as the beef. I worked my way through my portion listening to Pol and the magus go on discussing their campaign. I looked around for Sophos, but he was nowhere to be seen.

"I sent him after more wood," the magus broke off to tell me.

Knowing Sophos, I thought he had probably fallen in the river. "Can he swim?" I wondered out loud.

The magus glanced over at Pol, who shrugged his shoulders. Without another word they both stood up, brushed the sand off the seats of their trousers, and went to look for Sophos. Once they were gone, I flipped open Pol's bag and helped myself to another slab of dried beef, which I stuffed into one pocket. The magus would have given it to me if I had asked, I think, but I'd given up asking for extra food since the scene with the riding crop.

Sophos came over the ridge behind me, bringing a bundle of brush. "Where is everybody?"

"Looking for you." I explained that they thought he'd drowned.

He sat in huffy silence for the next half hour until the magus came up the riverbank from downstream. When he saw Sophos, he stepped back around the curve in the bank and must have waved to Pol because both of them reappeared.

They sat down beside us, and Sophos, staring straight ahead, said pointedly, "I swim very well."

"Is there any dinner?" I asked.

So we ate and waited for the river to disappear. I had moved away from the fire to sit in the dark. Sophos moved with me.

"Gen," he asked, "can you hear the river coming inside the temple?"

I thought about my panic on the previous two nights. Maybe my ears heard what my head didn't understand. "I don't know," I had to answer, and told him about the panic. I told him about the sliding stone door blocks as well.

"Do you think," he stammered, "there's some . . . body in the maze with you?"

I wished he hadn't so obviously substituted "somebody" for "something." Not that I thought ghouls and ghosts were real, but they were easier to believe in when standing in a cold, dark, wet hole in the ground.

My third night in the maze I remembered to pick up the pry bar, lying abandoned in the entranceway to the maze. Then I went directly to the corridor through the middle of it. I searched fingertip by fingertip every stretch of its inner wall from one end of it to the other, and then as nearly as I could tell, I circled through the maze to the far side of the same wall and searched it, too. It took most of my night, and I found nothing. I went to the pool in the back of the maze and waded through it, bones occasionally crunching under my feet despite my care. I searched the rear wall of the maze and again found nothing.

As I searched, Sophos's unspoken words came to haunt me, ". . . something in the maze with you?" I broke off every few minutes to look over my shoulder and cursed Sophos for bringing up something I didn't want to think about.

The flame in my lamp sputtered once, and the panic swept down on me. I went back to the middle corridor and stood there while the panic rolled over me, sweeping and pushing me toward the exit of the maze. I knew that there was still time before the maze filled, and I refused to admit defeat. I planted my feet and actually held on to the rock for support. I intended to find Hamiathes's Gift, and if I couldn't, or if as I suspected, it was not there to be found, I told myself that I might as well drown. What, after all, was there to go back to?

The panic receded, and I looked at the wall in front of me. There were bulges of rock and ripples where it had flowed and hardened, but there was no crack or fissure that would reveal a doorway or conceal a hidden spring. I searched through the middle section of the wall until frustration made me swear out loud and swing my pry bar against the solid rock.

I hurt my hand. The pry bar landed, ringing like a bell, on the stone at my feet. I was lucky it hadn't bounced off the rock and hit me in the face. I turned around and sat down against the wall, nursing my sore hand and wiping the tears off my face. The panic was gone, but I was still tempted to try to make my way out of the maze. I don't know if I could have left then or not. I didn't stay because I was trapped; I stayed because I was too stupid to go. Maybe all the owners of the bones in the back of the maze had been drowned by their own stubbornness as well.

I was facing the giant piece of obsidian, and I wondered how many had sat there before me. The Hephestial glass was beautiful, reflecting the light of the lamp that was sitting beside me. My own reflection was there as well, distorted by the bumps and ridges in the obsidian. I watched the image of the burning flame for a moment, thinking again how much like a window at night the glass was, reflecting the houselights when the world was dark, keeping the world on the far side of the glass invisible. How much like a window—or like a door.

I stood up, forgetting my sore hand. The piece of obsidian was easily the size of a double doorway, although veins of solid rock ran through it. I brushed my hands over the slick black surface and pressed my nose against it, trying to see through. There was nothing but blackness. I picked up my pry bar and, holding my breath, slammed it into the glass.

The pry bar rebounded, chipping free a small chunk of the obsidian. I turned my face away and swung again harder. Larger pieces of glass broke off, and when I turned back, there were long cracks radiating in a star shape from where the point of my pry bar had struck, and there, where the cracks intersected, was a little hole no bigger than a button. I pushed my fingertip through it, careful of the sharp edges, and wiggled it in the open space on the other side.

Turning my face again, I swung the pry bar over and over against the glass door until I felt something break loose and shatter on the stone floor. I looked and saw that a piece larger than an armored breastplate had dropped out and broken to fragments at my feet. There was dust in the air that stung my eyes. I lifted up my lamp to let light fall through the hole before me. There was no room beyond, but there was the space that my calculations had said must be behind the opposite wall of the corridor. I looked back for a moment, puzzled by my mistake. Then I looked again through the hole in the obsidian. There was a staircase, twelve steep steps, leading up. The room above was outside the range of my small light.

With more judicious taps of my pry bar I enlarged the opening between the veins of solid rock. Pieces of obsidian larger than platters broke off, and I lowered them carefully to the ground. Suddenly one tap of my hammer overcame the door all at once.

The veins of stone crumbled to fist-sized rocks, and a huge piece of glass slipped free and crashed down. Shards flew like missiles. I jumped back and covered my face with both arms. When the dust settled, I dropped my arms and looked through an irregular opening nearly as wide as a double doorway, to stairs that filled the space beyond. They were about eight feet wide, as the magus and my map had predicted. I had no idea, though, how they came to be on that side of the corridor, where the wall was only two feet thick.

I had dropped my lamp again, but it was still burning. I scooped it up and picked my way through the rubble of obsidian and stone and climbed up the stairs. The lamp was a round, fat one, a little longer than it was high, flat on the bottom, with two more flat spots on one side where I'd dropped it. It had a hint of a spout with a hole for the wick, but no handle. It sat in the palm of my hand, the brass growing warmer and less heavy as the oil inside burned away. There was very little oil left by then, and the lamp sat lightly. I held it above the level of my eyes so that it might cast its frugal glow ahead of me. There were no obstacles. I climbed with my eyes on the stairs, and so I did not realize until I reached the top and looked up that the room was filled with people.

They stood in a loose collection on either side of an open aisle. They were perfectly silent and none looked toward me, but it was impossible that they could be unaware of my arrival. The obsidian crashing to the floor had made enough sound to wake the dead, but no one moved. I was in plain sight, but no one looked at me. Finally I realized that the only movement in the entire room was the movement of the shadows thrown by my light as my hand shook, and I began to breathe again. They were statues.

As I walked among them, I could see that their perfection

made them unreal. Their skin was lighter or darker, but always unblemished, their faces symmetrical, their eyes clear. There were no scars, no bent limbs, no squints in those eyes. I wanted to touch the perfect skin, but I didn't dare. I settled for brushing my fingers across the cloth of one robe. It was deep blue and had a pattern like running water woven into it. The man wearing it was tall. Taller than I was, of course, but taller than the magus as well.

Away from the aisle, toward the back of the room, I found the woman in the white peplos. I knew her now, even without her feather pen and scroll, and I smiled in recognition. She was Moira, who recorded men's fates. How she had come to my dreams I didn't wonder. I had found her image in the world, and somehow I thought all mysteries were explained.

I left her and turned toward the altar but found that I was mistaken. There was no altar. There was a throne, and sitting on it was the statue of the Great Goddess Hephestia. She wore a robe cut from deep velvet, its reds darkest in the heart of its folds and brighter across the ridges. Her hair was held back from her face by a woven ribbon of gold set with red rubies. Resting on her knees was a small tray that held a single stone on its mirror surface. I stepped forward until I could reach to take the stone. Then, with my hand extended, I stopped, and was perfectly still as I watched the pattern of light on the velvet robe shift with the movement of a breath. My heart was like stone inside my chest.

This was not an image carefully made in imitation of Hephestia, amid a statuary garden of the gods. This was the Great Goddess, and she was surrounded by her court. My extended hand began to shake. I closed my eyes as I heard the rustle of cloth behind me, wondering if it was the midnight blue gown with the water pattern as Oceanus checked to see if I had left any dirt. I opened one eye and looked up at the Great Goddess. She looked beyond me, impassive, distant, not unaware of my presence but unmoved by it.

There was a murmur of voices behind me, but I made out no words. In the corner of my vision a figure moved forward. I hadn't seen him before, though I should have looked. His skin was not black like the Nimbians'. It was a deep brownish red, like fired clay, like that of the ancient people who'd left their portraits on the walls of the ruins on islands in the middle sea. His hair was dark like his half sister's, but her hair reflected the light in flashes of gold and auburn; his was black like charcoal. His face was much narrower, his nose sharper. On one cheek was a lighter scar of a burn mark, shaped like a rounded feather. He was smaller than the other gods, dressed in a tunic of plain gray.

"You have not yet offended the gods." Eugenides, the god who had once been mortal, spoke at last. "Except perhaps Aracthus, who was charged to let no thief enter here. Take the stone."

I did not move.

The patron of thieves came closer. He moved to his sister's right hand and laid his own across it.

"Take it," he said. His words were strangely accented, but not so very different from my way of speaking. The magus was not there to tell me how it compared with the language of the civilized world. I had no difficulty understanding the god's instruction. I just couldn't move.

My nerve had failed, I suppose. It wasn't so much that I was afraid of the retribution of lightning bolts that might follow. It was religion that had seeped into my childhood without my knowing it. The thought of stealing something from the Great Goddess was too awful to contemplate, and I could not do it.

Neither could I turn and flee. I was a little surprised at how stubborn I was turning out to be, but I wouldn't leave without the Gift. It mattered too much. Distantly I heard the swish and rattle of small stones as the water began to flow down the riverbed overhead, but I remained as immobile as the gods that I had mistaken for statues. Only my eyes moved as I looked from the small gray stone of the tray to the hand of Eugenides, to his face. And then, because I thought that if I were dying, I would do something that very few had done since the world was made, I looked again into the eyes of the Great Goddess, and for a moment she looked back at me. That was enough.

Released from my paralysis, I leaned forward a little further and plucked the stone off the mirrored tray. Then I turned and I ran. With the sound of water roaring in my ears, I ran for the staircase, past the gods, who watched impassively. I lifted my head only once to look for Moira, but she was hidden in the crowd.

When I reached the staircase, I jumped the first two steps and stumbled down the rest. I thumped against the wall across from the bottom step and dropped my lamp. I didn't stop to pick it up. After three nights in the maze I didn't need it. Brushing my hands against the walls, one with Hamiathes's Gift clutched in its fist, I ran on. When the wall on my left ended, I turned left, then right, and right again, then left, and left again, and splashed toward the doors which I had wedged open and which had again closed. I imagined Aracthus somewhere making a gesture, forcing a little more water through the bluff to move my blocks. He might yet succeed in trapping me. The water coming through the grille in the door washed against my legs, six inches deep. How many thieves, I wondered, had reached this point and still drowned? Would my bones end in the pool at the back of the maze? Would the obsidian door be restored and the Gift returned to its mirrored tray?

If I had dropped my tools, they would have disappeared into the water, but I did not fumble. The water beyond the door was twelve inches deep, and it was almost two feet deep before I reached the next door. I worked the lock and stepped back as the water forced the door open. In the antechamber the water was waist deep, and the waves made by the water thundering down in a solid pillar from the hole in the ceiling were as high as my chest. The pillar carried a glint of moonlight from above, but the chamber was as dark as the maze. I slid cautiously around, close to the walls, but I slipped at the top of the stair leading to the outer door and slid down underwater until I was pinned, unable to breathe, against the stone door.

I fought to turn over, to get some purchase in order to lift my head, but the river held me on my back, head down. I scrabbled with my hands but could find no leverage to move my body against the force of the water. The river foamed around me. I ran out of air. Darkness that was deeper than the river swallowed me up.

chapter 10

_W_HEN I WOKE, the sun was up and the day was already warm. I was on the sandy bank of the Aracthus, my feet still in the water. The river lifted them and tugged gently, but not as if it still hoped to suck me in. It was moving quietly between its banks and seemed willing to make peace over the loss of Hamiathes's Gift. At least that was my thinking as my eyes opened. A moment later came more sensible questions. Had I tried to escape the last maze at the last minute the night before and been trapped by the river, hallucinating everything else, the obsidian door, the gods, Hephestia, and Hamiathes's Gift?

Altogether they seemed to make a likely fantasy that would fit well with my dreams during the past week. I wondered if I could have invented the cloth on Oceanus's robe and the way it had felt, first satin cool and then velvet soft. My fingertips brushed against each other at the memory, and I looked down to see what I held in my hand. Still caught in my palm after a night in the river was the poor, plain, gray-and-white spotted stone—Hamiathes's Gift.

Covering that hand with the other, I closed my eyes and thanked Hephestia, and Eugenides, Oceanus, Moira, Aracthus, and every god and goddess I could remember. Then I pulled my feet out of the river and dragged myself up to where the sand was dry and lay down to sleep a little longer. The magus, Pol, and Sophos found me there. They had seen the stone door from the cliff lying in the clear water beyond the waterfall and had walked downstream with their packs in case they might find my body and give it a decent burial before turning toward home. I woke to find them standing around me.

"Well," the magus said when I rolled over, "that is good news at least." As I sat up, he leaned over me. "It is a great relief to my conscience that you are not drowned, Gen." He patted my shoulder awkwardly. "We are alive and you are alive, so this expedition was at least not the disaster of earlier ones. If we failed to retrieve Hamiathes's Gift, well, perhaps someone else found it first, or perhaps it was never there at all."

I had meant to make him wait a little, but he sounded so bleak that without meaning to, I rolled my hand over and opened the fist so that he could see the Gift, resting on my palm.

His knees seemed to weaken, and he squatted down beside me with his mouth open. I smiled at his wonder and my own delight. I was taken aback when he put his arms around my shoulders and hugged me like his own son, or anyway like a close relative.

"You are a wonder, Gen. I will carve your name on a stele outside the basilica, I promise."

I laughed out loud.

"Where was it?"

I told him about the obsidian door and the stairway to the

throne room, but I stumbled a little. When it came time to mention the gods, I passed over them. It didn't seem right to talk about them in the light of day, with people who didn't believe and might laugh. If the magus noticed, he didn't comment.

"The river came down just as you said it might," he told me. "And washed right across our campsite on the lower bank. So we owe you for our lives as well as for this." He looked down at the stone he held in his hand.

"Is that really it?" Sophos asked. "How can you tell?"

The magus flipped it over so that he could see the lettering carved there, the four symbols of Hephestia's ancient name.

"But it's just a plain gray rock," said Sophos.

"Do you have any doubts?" I asked.

"No," Sophos admitted. "I just don't understand why I am so sure."

"In the story the other night," I told Sophos, "when Hephestia rewarded Hamiathes at the end, she was supposed to have taken an ordinary stone from the river and dipped it in the water of immortality."

"So it is just a rock?" he asked.

"Not entirely," said the magus. "Look carefully at it in the sun." He handed it back to me. I bounced it a moment on my palm. It was a rounded oval and just the weight, I thought, to go in a slingshot. But I looked closer at the letters carved in the side of it and saw the sun glint off something blue at the bottom of the carving.

"It's a sapphire," I said, "at least part of it is." I peered down the hole bored from top to bottom, then flipped it over and, looking closely, could see where the water had worn the stone smooth and uncovered a few blue flecks of the gem inside.

"There is a description of it in the scrolls of the high priests of Eddis," said the magus. "Whenever anyone produced a stone, the high priest compared it to the scroll's description. No one but the priest could read the description, and so no one ever offered a successful copy. Probably because someone who is already as wealthy and powerful as the high priest of Eddis is difficult to corrupt."

"Or he's corrupt already and doesn't want to share his power," I said.

"But you know the description?" Sophos said to the magus.

"Yes."

"How?" I asked.

"My predecessor visited the high priest during a trip as ambassador to Eddis. He offered the priest a drugged bottle of wine and then looked through his library while he was unconscious. He didn't think that the description of the stone was particularly important at the time, but I found it noted in his journals after he disappeared."

I shuddered at the idea of poisoning a high priest. For that sort of crime they were still throwing people off the edge of the mountain.

"You're wet, Gen," said the magus, mistaking the cause of my shivers. "Get into some dry clothes and get something to eat. Then if you have the strength, I'd like to get at least partway across the dystopia. The rest of our food is with Ambiades."

So I ate the last of the jerky. The bread was gone. Sophos filled a cup with river water for me and set it aside until the silt settled. I had once again lost the tie for my hair, so I asked Pol for some string. He offered me two pieces of leather thong, one longer than the other. I tied up the end of my braid with the long one and kept the short one to use later. Then we began to pick our way back across the dystopia, the magus wearing Hamiathes's Gift around his neck. It had passed out of my hands only a few hours after I had stolen it.

When the sun got hot in the middle of the day, we crawled into the shade of the tilted rocks and slept for a few hours. We reached the edge of the olive trees as the sun was setting, but we were still more than a mile above the campsite where we had left Ambiades. The sky was light as we walked south, but the groves were dark. Through the darkness we saw Ambiades's fire blazing.

The magus shook his head. "He'll have the fire watch out from fifty miles away." He sent Pol ahead to put it out, or at least reduce the blaze, so that when the magus, Sophos, and I got to the clearing, Ambiades was over the first shock of seeing us return alive.

"I thought you were all dead," he said. He didn't admit that he'd kept the fire burning bright because he'd been afraid of our ghosts wandering back across the dystopia. While we were gone, he'd eaten most of the food, but the magus spared him any lectures, and we all went to sleep. I didn't wake to see if anyone was keeping watch over me. I didn't stir until the sun was up and I heard Ambiades moving around the camp, cleaning up the mess he'd made while we were gone. There was nothing for breakfast.

The magus intended to go down the edge of the Sea of Olives until we reached the nearest town to buy food for ourselves as well as some for the horses. "We'll take a more direct route home. Now that we have the Gift, the quicker we go the better," he said.

The horses must have been as happy as I was about the prospect of fresh food. The grazing was poor among the dried-up grasses. We packed up and rode back into the olives until we came to the overgrown maintenance road that turned toward the distant Seperchia. We came to a wide, shallow stream. As our horses stepped into the water, a group of mounted men swung out from behind a patch of dry oak and brambles where they had been hidden. I saw that they had swords in their hands. I didn't wait to learn anything else.

The magus and I were nearly knee to knee, ahead of the others. I dragged the reins of my horse over to one side, and it stumbled into the horse beside it. I brushed shoulders with the magus for just a moment and then turned the horse on its haunches and drove it with my heels back toward the trees on the streambank. As a branch passed overhead, I grabbed it, using my free hand, and pulled myself up into the tree.

By the time I was secure on a higher branch and could look down, Pol and the magus had their swords out and one of the attacking horsemen was already lying in the water. I watched as the magus proved himself to be a swordsman as dangerous as Pol. Between them they held the three remaining attackers. Sophos was behind them, twisted in the saddle, his back to the fight, trying to get his own sword out of his saddlebag. Ambiades was doing the same, but he'd had the sense to first run his horse onto the bank, away from danger. Sophos, looking in the wrong direction, didn't know how close he was to being spitted.

I called his name, but he couldn't hear me over the other shouting, which in retrospect I realized was mostly the magus and Pol yelling at him to forget the sword and hide in the trees. Pol was being drawn out by one attacker, leaving the magus to fight two men and Sophos still unaware of his danger. His attention was on his sword belt, which was caught in the buckle of his saddlebag.

Swearing, I stood up on my tree branch and rushed along its length. I threw myself facedown, lying mostly on the main limb and partly on the outer branches, and reached through the prickling leaves. All that I could reach of Sophos was his hair. I grabbed that and pulled him off-balance just as a horseman slipped between the magus and Pol.

Sophos fell face first off his horse, almost taking me with him. He landed in the mud with his horse between him and the fighting, and if he'd stayed down, he would have been safe, but he struggled to his feet, sword in hand, as the cursed horse moved away. He was left standing with his mouth open, looking at the lifted sword of his opponent.

I closed my eyes, but at the last possible moment he must have shifted his weight and parried the blow aimed at his head. His return to guard position was slow, and I don't know what he would have done next, being too far off-balance to recover, but he didn't need to do anything. As I opened my eyes, Pol slid his sword into the man's rib cage, nearly to the hilt. The man grunted and hung for a moment on the sword before he slid off into the water. There was another splash on the far side of the stream as the magus finished his opponent as well. I pushed myself upright on my branch and moved back toward the trunk of the tree.

There were four riderless horses, stamping around in the muddy stream. When their feet stopped crunching on the gravel and they stood still, looking confused, the magus was able to ask Sophos if he was hurt.

"No, I'm fine."

"Good. Ambiades?"

"I'm fine."

"Pol?"

"Nothing serious." He was mopping up blood from a slice just below his elbow.

"And Gen? I see you found a safe place to wait while we were busy."

I opened my mouth to point out that I didn't have a sword to defend myself with, not that I wouldn't have climbed the tree anyway, but instead I stared at him with my mouth hanging open like a horrified gargoyle. I pointed to his shirt. He lifted one hand, instinctively checking for a wound, before he realized. Hamiathes's Gift was gone. He looked down at the neatly sliced leather thong lying over one shoulder. He ran his hand over it in disbelief, then felt frantically in the folds of his clothes. He checked the ridges in his saddle and saddlebags before he jumped off his horse and waded into the stream, cursing. Pol and Sophos followed after him, but there was too much mud in the water by then. Nothing could be seen.

"What happened? What happened?" cried Ambiades from the bank. He was the only one of us still mounted.

"The stone, the cursed stone," said the magus. "I've lost it in the fighting. Damn it, who the hell are these people?" he said, shifting a body off a gravel bank in midstream.

"Are they all dead?" Ambiades asked.

"Yes, they're all dead. Get over here and help me with this one."

They dragged the bodies out of the water, while I sat forgotten in the tree. I very carefully rebraided my hair and watched. When the dead men were laid out on the bank, the magus remembered me.

"Come down and help look," he told me. He was distracted and was asking more than ordering.

Reluctantly I slipped down from the tree and stepped around the bodies. They were soldiers of the queen of Attolia. One of them was a lieutenant. He was young, and looked younger with wet hair stuck to his forehead and water beading on his face. He'd led the other horsemen as they rode down on us, led them no doubt onto the end of Pol's sword.

There was one part of his uniform that hadn't gotten wet, with either blood or water, and its shape—a coleus leaf—caught my eye. After a moment I stooped to scoop a little water from the stream and dribbled it back and forth across the dry spot on his tunic. I soaked the image until it melted into the wetness of the rest of his uniform. The water was cold. It splashed on his neck and pooled in the hollow of his collarbone, but he didn't mind, and he didn't deserve to be marked with the coward leaf as he journeyed to the underworld.

When the mark was gone, I straightened up and noticed Pol watching me. I shrugged and wiped my hands on my pants, but my pants were muddy and my hands only ended up dirty as well as wet.

We left the bodies lying on the bank while the magus organized a search for Hamiathes's Gift. Once the mud had settled, he had us stand in a line across the stream well below where the fighting had been. Staying in line, we worked our way upstream until he was sure we had passed the place where the stone would have dropped. There wasn't enough current to have moved the stone far, but the stone was no different from any of the thousands of pebbles there on the streambed. Only the magus and I had held the stone. Ambiades had never even seen it. We'd stayed for almost a quarter of an hour, all of us staring at the gravel under our feet when Pol finally spoke up.

"It's gone, magus."

The rest of us continued to stare at the streambed.

"Magus." Pol spoke more firmly, and this time we picked up our heads. Ambiades, Sophos, and I looked back and forth between the magus and his soldier.

"Yes," the magus finally agreed, after a long moment of silence. "We've got to go. Ambiades, get the horses and bring them to this side of the stream. Sophos, see if any of those other horses are still nearby. We should have tied them up. If they have saddlebags, check to see if there's any food in them."

Three of the horses were standing with ours—misery loves company—but the fourth one was gone, presumably back to its camp.

"There's no time to catch it now," said the magus. "We'll have to go as quickly as we can." He pulled himself onto his horse and looked one last time at the stream. "I don't believe this," he said.

I watched him until even I felt uncomfortable and looked away, as Pol, Sophos, and Ambiades had done. He'd had the stone for a day and lost it; I should have been pleased. Five days earlier I would have been delighted to imagine what it would be like for him in the court of Sounis when he went back to his king and told him the gamble had failed, but I wasn't enjoying myself. I told myself it was because I was wet from wading in the stream. Or it may have been that I was afraid of the people who would be coming soon to find out what happened to the lieutenant and his three men.

"All right," said the magus at last. "All right. Let's go." But he still didn't turn his horse away from the stream. In the distance we heard a shout. The stray horse had been found, but the magus sat, unwilling to give up. He looked at the streambank and the trees around him, as if for landmarks, as if there were some hope that he might return to the place to search again. My nerves communicated themselves to my horse, and it sidled and blew underneath me.

Finally the magus dragged himself away. We turned our horses down the track and kicked them into a gallop. The magus rode beside me, still looking stunned. I don't know what the others were thinking; I was concentrating on my riding. This was no time to drop behind or, worse, fall off the horse.

When we'd covered some distance, we turned into the trees and rode more slowly for almost an hour until we came to another open path.

"They'll track us," Sophos said, looking over his shoulder.

"We'll have to keep ahead of them," said the magus. I swiveled my head around to look at him. He sounded almost cheerful. He looked cheerful.

"A little danger adds spice to life, Gen," he told me.

I was stunned at his recovery, and it must have shown. "I've had some time to think, Gen. The stone itself isn't important. Now that we have seen it for ourselves, as well as having the description, and we know that no one else can produce the original, we can make a copy."

How someone could have held that stone in his hand and then say it wasn't important, I didn't know. I almost expected lightning to strike him dead.

"What about the fact that the stone is supposed to carry its own authority?" I snapped. "You're supposed to look at it and know that it is Hamiathes's Gift." We'd all felt that, I'd thought, by the banks of the Aracthus.

But the magus had an answer. "That will be dismissed as superstition," he said confidently. "We'll manage. We'll manage just fine."

All of my work could be thrown away. He would *manage*. I gritted my teeth.

The magus turned to speak to Pol. "We'll follow this track into the cultivated groves, then cut through those toward the main road. If they haven't seen us, we might hide in traffic; if they have, we'll swing back under the olives and use the maintenance paths as much as possible."

"What about food?" I asked. My tone nettled him.

"I guess we'll try to get something in Pirrhea tonight," he said vaguely.

"Tonight?" My exasperation pierced his bubble of false cheer.

"I'm sorry," he snapped, "but I can't pull food out of the sky for you."

"You're not going to pull it out of Pirrhea either," I said. "What do you plan to do, knock on a door and say, 'Excuse us, there are four of the Queen's Guard dead, soldiers are searching every road for us, and I'd like to buy a few loaves of bread and some dried beef, please'?"

"And what do you suggest, O oracle of the gutter?"

"I suggest that you should have brought food for five people with this miserable traveling circus of yours. Alternatively, you should have left Useless the Elder and his younger brother at home!"

"He's not my brother." Ambiades was offended.

"That," I snarled at him, "was a figure of speech. Now shut up." He jumped in the saddle as if he'd been slapped. I turned back to the magus. "How do you propose to get food?"

But the magus had had a moment to think and had arrived at the obvious solution. "You," he said, "are going to steal it."

I threw up my hands.

Pirrhea was an old town. Like many, it had outgrown its walls and was surrounded by fields and farmhouses. I walked through kitchen gardens, harvesting whatever my hands found in the dark. I dropped what I gathered into a bag I had taken from a shed at the first house I passed. Once I got too close to a goat pen and the occupants bleated at me. When no one came out to check on them, I went in and collected two cans of goat milk from the settling shelf. I was thirsty as well as hungry and drank one of the cans while I considered burgling someone's kitchen for leftover bread. I decided against it. Stale bread wasn't worth the risk, but I did slip into the henhouse of the largest home I passed, to wring the necks of three chickens. I dropped them into a second bag and left town.

The magus and the others were waiting for me in the trees on the far side of an onion field. I hadn't been keen to risk my neck for them. There had been recriminations of uselessness as we rode. Ambiades hadn't liked it when I'd suggested he should have been left home. I pointed out that he'd been no help at the ford. He pointed out that I had climbed a tree. I pointed out that I had no sword. He offered to give me his, point first.

When I'd left the others in a rare grove of almond trees outside town, the magus had told me he'd give me an hour, and if I wasn't back by then, he'd find the town center and shout "Thief!" at the top of his lungs.

In the dark he hadn't been able to see the contempt on my face, but he could hear it in my voice. "Be sure to shout 'Murderers! Murderers!' too," I said.

His answer had followed me as I walked away. "I'll make sure that we all go to the block together."

Everyone looked sadly at the chickens when the magus said there was no time to cook them. Pol tied them to his saddle, and we headed off into the dark, eating handfuls of raw vegetables and crunching grit in our teeth.

"There's a livery stable on the main road at Kahlia," the magus said. "We can steal a change of horses there."

I choked on the spinach I was chewing. "We can what?"

"It's another two hours' ride if we push the horses." He went on, ignoring my interruption. "We can find a place to camp by the road. There are enough travelers that we won't be noticed. We'll get a couple of hours' sleep. Pol, you could put the chickens into the fire, and then we'll get the horses and ride on. We should lose them when we cut away from the main road, away from the Seperchia's pass to Eddis. They won't expect that."

"You are going to use the same trail back home? Why not just ride for the main pass?" Ambiades asked. "It's closer, isn't it? And once we're in Eddis, we're on neutral ground."

"Once we get to Kahlia we'd be closer to the main pass," the magus agreed. "But they'll have all the roads blocked, and I'm not sure we could sneak through. The land around the pass is mostly open fields. They won't expect us to cut back inland, and we should slip by them."

"I think the main pass would be better," Ambiades said hesitantly, giving the magus one last chance.

"It's not your job to think," the magus told him.

Ambiades tossed his head, and I thought he might say something, but he didn't.

"About those horses . . ." I said.

"You'll do your best, Gen," said the magus, "and if your best isn't good enough, we'll all—"

"Go to the block together," I grumbled. "You said that before."

No one said anything more until we stopped on the road just outside Kahlia. The magus was as optimistic as ever. Pol seemed to take everything in stride, and Sophos didn't know enough to be frightened. Only Ambiades was as nervous as a cat too close to a fire. Sophos had forgotten that he was keeping his distance from his idol, and he tried to chat with Ambiades as they unsaddled the horses, but Ambiades didn't answer.

Pol kindled a fire in a traveler's fire ring and cut up the chickens to cook. The fire ring was just a circle of stones mortared together. There was one every fifty yards or so on the roads outside large towns. They were built for the merchants who stopped their packtrains outside towns to camp. There were several packtrains camped near us that night, and smaller groups of travelers with just one wagon or no wagon at all. It was warm enough that a tent or a blanket roll would do. There were a few guards posted, but they weren't watching for us.

We all slept, except Pol. The magus woke me before he woke the others and gave me careful directions how to get through town to the livery stable near the opposite gate.

"Bring the horses out there. Pol will be waiting for you. The rest of us will be up the road with the saddles." He seemed as carefree as Sophos, but he didn't have Sophos's excuse.

"Do you have any idea how impossible this is?" I asked him.

He laughed. "I thought you said you could steal anything." He gave me a shove on the shoulder and started me down the road.

"Things," I hissed to myself as I walked, "don't make noise."

The moon was still up, and there was enough light to see the road in front of me. When I got close to the town walls, I could see by the light of lanterns burning by the gates. They were open. They probably hadn't been closed for years, but there was a guard in the archway.

He was supposed to be watching for suspicious people—like me. I couldn't think of a plausible excuse for coming into town at such an hour, so I avoided the problem altogether by circling away from the gate and climbing over the wall out of the guard's sight. I dropped down into someone's backyard, then worked my way between buildings until I found a wide street that I hoped was the one the magus had mentioned in his directions.

I hurried through absolutely empty intersections, listening at every corner for the footsteps of the watch, but I met no one. I was on the right street, and I found the livery stable and the inn next to it without trouble. Both were closed for the night of course. Wooden shutters were pulled over the windows of the inn, and the gates to the courtyard were closed. I listened again for the watch, and when I heard nothing, I pushed open one gate after lifting its post off the ground so that it wouldn't scrape. The post fit into a gap between the flagstones so that the gate wouldn't swing closed again.

When I peeped into the stable, I found the ostler asleep in his chair at one end. Good luck for me. Not only was he asleep, but I guessed by the empty bottle on his left that he was drunk as well. I collected five leading straps from a peg over his head and slipped down the row of stalls, looking into each one at a sleeping horse. I picked five that I thought were mares and woke them with a whisper. I clipped the straps to their halters, and then I opened all the stall doors, carefully so that there was no squeak, starting with the one farthest from the ostler. The horses lifted themselves to their feet. Puzzled at being disturbed at such an odd hour, they made small noises of inquiry, none loud enough to wake the ostler.

When all the stall doors were open, I went back to my chosen five and led the first one out. As I led her past the stall of my next choice, I leaned in to twitch the strap hanging from that mare's halter. She obediently followed her stablemate out of the stall and down the row. The other horses came out in the same way. Soon all five were in a line, and the horses left in their stalls were leaning out of their stalls, wondering what they were missing.

I was at the door of the stable, looking out at the stone-flagged courtyard where the horses' hooves were going to sound like the crack of doom. I looked back at the sleeping ostler. He would sleep through the noise only if he were very drunk indeed, and there was no way to know how much had been in the bottle when he started. There was an obvious solution, but I was a thief, not yet a murderer.

I sent a hasty prayer to the god of thieves that the horses would keep quiet and that the ostler was blind drunk; then I shuffled around until I had all five leading ropes in my hands and drew the horses out.

The silence was so profound that I turned back to make sure that the horses were following. It hadn't occurred to me that the gods that I'd seen silent and unmoving in their temple might still be taking an interest in me. I almost bumped into the mare directly behind me. She threw up her head in surprise but didn't make a noise. I stepped backward, and she followed. The iron shoes on her hooves struck the flagstones soundlessly. The other horses came as well. Afraid that I'd been struck deaf, I backed out of the courtyard. Behind my horses came the others from the stable. They slipped through the gates of the inn and disappeared like ghosts down different streets. When the ostler woke, he would have to search the entire town before he would know that five of his charges were missing.

At the town gate I found Pol standing over the body of a guard.

"Did you kill him?" My lips formed the words without speaking.

Pol shook his head. Like the ostler, the guard was asleep. Pol took four of the horses, two leading straps in each hand, and left me just one to lead up the grass beside the road, between two houses and then out across the fields. We reached the cover of some trees and found the other three waiting.

"Was there any trouble?" the magus asked, and the spell of silence burst with a pop.

I shook my head. "No," I said, "no trouble." Except that I'd discovered that I was eager to divest myself of the gods' attention as quickly as possible.

Sophos took the leading strap from my hands and led my horse away to be saddled.

Pol asked me, "Are you all right?"

I nodded my head.

He took me by the elbow and felt my body shaking. "Are you sure?"

I nodded again. How could I explain that this was a perfectly normal reaction for someone who has had a careless prayer answered by the gods? The silence of the horses had been immeasurably more unnerving than the gods in their temple.

Maybe because the stables had been part of my world and the temple had not. I don't know. For the first time in a long while, Pol had to help me onto my horse.

We were only an hour away from Kahlia when a cold, damp breeze blew down my neck and I pulled up my horse to listen to the sound of the temple gong beating in the night.

"What's that?" Ambiades asked when the others had also stopped.

Probably Aracthus, still doing his part, I thought. "The ostler woke up," I said, and dug my heels into the horse underneath me.

By morning we had nearly covered the ground back to the mountain trail. The horses were exhausted, and our pursuers were so close that twice we'd seen them over our shoulders at straight places in the road. The ostler must have called out the town garrison without counting his horses first. We lost sight of the soldiers when we turned into the olive groves, but they remained close behind. As we twisted in the dark under the trees, we moved a little quicker than our pursuers, only because we knew where we were going and they did not.

The mountain rose so steeply out of the Sea of Olives that it appeared without warning as we came out of the trees. Suddenly in front of us sunshine was falling on the piled rubble at the base of the cliff. The magus pulled up his horse and dismounted.

"Not many people know about the trail. If we can get up the cliffside before they see us, they might not know where we've gone."

"Doesn't Eddis begin here? Won't we be on neutral ground?" Sophos asked.

"Only if there're enough Eddisians to insist on it," said the magus, and slapped his horse with the riding crop, sending it down the alley between trees and mountains, followed by the other horses. "Get moving," he said to the rest of us.

"Not me," I said, intending to find a safe hiding place to wait until the hunt flowed past. It was past time for me to be going my own way. Once they were free of pursuit, the magus and Pol might turn their attention to ensuring my return to Sounis and prison, and I wasn't going back to prison, or to Sounis for that matter.

The magus was astonished. Then he was angry. "What do you mean, not you?"

"I'm not going back to prison or the silver mines or some other hole in the ground. I'll take my chances in Attolia."

"You think I would take you back to the prison?" the magus asked.

"You think I would trust you?" I answered, unfairly. He hadn't given me any reason not to trust him, but everyone remembered my comments in the mountains about the probability of a knife in the back.

"The Attolians will kill you just the same," he said, "more painfully probably."

"They'll be too busy chasing you."

The magus glanced over at Pol.

"You don't have time to waste forcing me," I pointed out.

He threw up his hands. "Fine!" he bellowed. "Go die on the swords of the Attolians. Be drawn, be quartered, be hung, I don't care. Spend the rest of your life in one of their dungeons. What possible difference would it make to me?"

I sighed. I hadn't intended to offend him. "Leave me a sword," I said without thinking, "and I'll do my best to slow them down." I could have bitten off my own tongue, but the magus didn't take me up on my offer. He snorted in disbelief and turned away.

The others followed, but Sophos turned back after a few hesitant steps. He awkwardly pulled his sword free from its scabbard and offered it hilt first in my direction. "It's not any use to me," he explained truthfully.

It was a beginner's sword, lighter than a regular one but better than nothing. I took it by the blunt part of the blade just below the hilt and raised it to him before he turned to hurry after the magus, who had looked back once to snort in contempt before disappearing between the boulders.

I chose a nearby boulder and climbed up the side of it. Once I reached the top, I was above the eye level of any passing horseman, and it was as good a hiding place as any. Any pursuers would ride by without being aware of me, unless of course I jumped down on them, waving a sword.

I couldn't imagine what had possessed me to suggest such a thing to the magus. I'd sworn to the gods from the king's prison that I wasn't going to embroil myself in any more stupid plans. Of course I hadn't actually believed in the gods at the time, but why should I care what happened to the magus and his apprentices? I spent ten minutes sweating in the sun, reviewing all the reasons I didn't like the magus and everything he stood for, and trying to ignore a grisly image of all of them being beheaded.

There was a jingle of bits, and several hundred yards away the Attolians appeared one by one from the cover of the trees. They paused to look at the hoofprints leading toward the main pass, then ignored them, riding directly toward the magus's secret trail. They weren't the garrison from Kahlia; like the soldiers we'd met earlier, they were dressed in the colors of the Queen's Guard.

I told myself one more time as they passed beneath me that the only reasonable thing to do was to wait until they passed, so I could sneak down the far side of the boulder and disappear into the trees. Then I jumped onto the shoulders of the second rider from the front. The other horses were moving too quickly to stop, and as I hit the ground on top of the Attolian, I saw a hoof land on the turf several inches from the end of my nose. The Attolian struggled up on top of me, just in time to be hit by a following hoof. The horse came down as I scrambled away on all fours, dragging Sophos's sword. I'd managed not to stick the Attolian, his horse, or myself. I got to my feet and ran.

Once I was among the olives I could move faster than the men still on horses, and I was well ahead of those who'd been thrown. I was heading for a patch of dry oaks I'd seen from the clifftop ten days earlier. The oaks grew low to the ground, and I counted on their tightly packed leaves to hide me. Without dogs, the pursuers had little chance of dragging me out and I could stay undercover until nightfall, then disappear in the dark.

The solid mass of oak trees was visible between the trunks of the olives, and I was slowing down, trying to pick the best place to dive into the cover of their leaves, when a second party of horsemen appeared and cut off my escape. Unable to outdistance them for long, I swung back toward the mountain, hoping to get among the rocks, where I couldn't be ridden down. If I could climb the cliff face, and if they didn't have crossbows or, gods forbid it, guns to shoot me with, I might get away or at least surrender without being killed first. I pounded across the hard-packed dirt under the olives, and some small part of me that should have been thinking something more sensible noticed that my strength had returned since I'd left the king's prison.

I made it to open ground, but my pursuers caught up with me just before I reached the rocks. A horse moved in front of me, and I had to turn to avoid it. There were horses everywhere, and shouting. Everyone seemed to be shouting.

chapter 11

*I* HEARD THE tumblers clicking as the guards unlocked my cell door before opening it to wave the magus in. Without turning my head, I could see him silhouetted in the doorway with Sophos beside him. Once the door was closed and locked behind him, the cell was dark. I lay quietly and hoped that he hadn't seen me.

"Magus?" Sophos whispered.

"Yes, I saw," the magus answered, and my hopes sank. I heard him taking small, careful steps across the floor. When he got close to me, he squatted down and reached out with his hands. One of them brushed my leg and then my sleeve and followed it down my arm until he touched my hand very quickly, to see if I was warm and alive or cold and dead.

"He's alive," he told Sophos as he put his hand back over mine and squeezed it. It was meant to be comforting.

"Gen, can you hear me?" he whispered softly.

"Go away."

In the dark he found my face and pushed the hair that had been lying across it out of the way. He was very gentle. "Gen, I owe you an apology. I'm sorry."

I didn't answer. Only a short time before, I had floated to the surface of the pain that had swallowed me up. I didn't care much about his apology.

Sophos kneeled down beside me in the dark. "How did you get here?" he whispered, as if the guard were lurking outside to hear the prisoners' conversation.

"They had a cart."

The magus snorted. His fingers left my face, and I felt them lightly touching the front of my shirt where it was stiff with dried blood. "Don't," I said. My voice was wispy and thin. I tried to pull myself together and started again. "Just leave me alone. I'm fine. Go away."

"Gen, I think the bleeding has stopped. I've still got my cloak. I'm going to see if I can wrap you in it."

"No," I said, "no, no, no." I didn't dare shake my head, but I desperately didn't want the magus to try to wrap me in his cloak. I didn't want his cloak. I didn't want him to put his hand beneath my head and lift it to slide Sophos's fancy folded cloak underneath, which is what he did first. When he didn't notice the bump under my hair at the base of my skull, I gave up protesting. The pain washed back over me, and I sank into it. The last thing I heard was the magus arguing with a guard about clean water and bandages.

When I woke again, there was a gloomy light coming through the cell's barred window, and I could see Sophos hovering. My shirt had been opened, and I was wrapped in white bandages. The magus must have won his argument.

Sophos saw me looking cross-eyed down at my chest and said, "He told the guard that you could always be killed later, but if you were dead, you couldn't be questioned by anyone but the gods."

That was comforting. "Where is everyone?" I asked.

He came to sit cross-legged beside me. I was lying on his cloak and wrapped in the magus's. "They came an hour ago and took the magus away," he said. "Pol and Ambiades are dead. The queen's soldiers were waiting for us at the top of the cliff. Ambiades had told them about the trail."

He waited, and when I couldn't think of anything to say, he told me, "We saw everything from the top of the cliff."

Hence the magus's apology.

The captain of the Queen's Guard and his men had been waiting on the mountainside. No doubt they had had more men stationed at the entrance to the Seperchia Pass, but the captain had gambled on the magus's leaving Attolia the way he had come in. When Pol and the magus boosted Sophos over the lip, he'd seen their boots, but he'd been dragged onto the clifftop before he could shout a warning. There had been nothing the magus and Pol could do but follow with Ambiades. When the captain of the guard had asked where I was, the magus, still angry at me, had said, "Saving his own skin." Stretched flat on top of the boulder, I was easy to see from above.

"He's planning an ambush," said one of the soldiers, and raised a crossbow.

"The queen wanted them all alive," the captain reminded him.

"Then don't bother to shoot him," the magus said bitterly. "He'll hide there until you climb down to arrest him."

"He's armed," said the captain, and he cupped his hands to his mouth to shout a warning to his men but lowered them when the magus fluttered one hand in dismissal. "The only thing he can do with a sword is steal it or sell it."

So they stood and watched me turn an orderly hunt into a knot of fallen horses and wounded men. The captain swung toward the magus, who was clearly stunned, and then changed his mind about what he was going to say. "Not what you expected?" he asked in wry tones.

The magus shook his head, watching me as I ran for cover.

"My men will cut him off," the captain assured him as I disappeared under the olives.

"He's done for," said Ambiades when I was chased back into the open by the horsemen. "Good riddance," he added as they bore down on me.

"Shut up, Ambiades," the magus said.

"They'll have to dismount to get him," said the captain.

"They won't have any trouble," the magus had said sadly, not knowing how strongly my father had desired me to become a soldier and not a thief.

"I've never seen someone win against that many men," said Sophos, sitting on the cold stone floor beside me.

"You still haven't," I pointed out. "Tell me about Ambiades." I didn't want to talk about the fight at the base of the mountains. Something unpleasant had happened. I couldn't remember exactly what it was. I didn't want to.

But Sophos wouldn't be distracted. "No, I suppose not. But you wounded two of them, and I think you killed the last one."

My eyes closed. That was what I hadn't wanted to think about. I hadn't intended to kill anyone, but I'd panicked when I'd seen swords on every side.

"We saw you run back into the open," Sophos went on mercilessly. "Why didn't they ride you down?"

"Too many rocks," I whispered. I was tired. "And they were riding farm horses. They only step on people by accident."

Only four of the soldiers had dismounted at first. I'd chopped one of them on the forearm, then disarmed another and gotten my sword tangled in his hilt. I wouldn't have been able to free a longer sword, but I managed to pull Sophos's clear in time to stop a thrust from someone on my left. Training that I thought I'd forgotten turned the block into a lunge, and I'd sunk the sword into my opponent, certainly killing him. It had felt no different from stabbing a practice dummy. I was so horrified that as he fell away from me, I'd let the sword slip out of my hand. I hadn't wanted to be a soldier. I'd become a thief instead, to avoid the killing. See where that had gotten me.

A light push from behind had forced me forward a half step. When I looked down, my shirt was lifted away from my chest like a tent, with a half inch of sword poking through a tear in the cloth. The point must have entered somewhere around the middle of my back but had slanted to come out near my armpit. I remembered very clearly that there was only a smear of blood on the steel.

"We thought you were dead," Sophos told me.

So had I. My knees had folded. Things were muddled and awful for a long time, and when I opened my eyes again, I was lying on my back and the sky over me was perfectly blue. The blue was all I could see. I must have been on a cart, but its sides were out of my sight. There was no sign of olive trees or the mountains. If it hadn't been for the jolting as the cartwheels turned, I could have been lying on a cloud. People still seemed to be shouting, but they were very far away. They were important people, shouting about me. I heard the king of Sounis and the queen of Eddis and other voices I couldn't identify. I thought that they might be gods. I wanted to tell them not to fuss. I wanted to explain that I would be dead soon, and there would be nothing left to fuss over, but the cart must have hit a particularly severe bump. The blue sky above me turned to red and then to black.

*   *   *

Sophos dragged me out of the memory, asking, "Who taught you to fight like that?"

"My father."

"Was he very angry when you turned out to be a thief?"

I thought of the fight when I'd torn up my enrollment papers for the army. "Yes." Still, we'd gotten much closer once the matter was settled and done with. "But he's used to it now."

"You should have been a soldier," Sophos said. "You were better than Ambiades ever was. I think that's why he said, 'Good riddance,' again, and that's when Pol—" Sophos stopped.

I opened my eyes to see that he was crying. He scrubbed his sleeve across his face to wipe away some of the snot and tears. I hadn't wanted to think about what had happened at the bottom of the cliff, and Sophos hadn't wanted to think about what had happened at the top.

He wiped away some more tears and, after a few deep breaths, continued quietly. "The magus told Ambiades that there was nothing to be pleased about, and the captain of the guard said yes, there was, and Ambiades just looked kind of sick at first, like the magus, but then he started to look pleased with himself. And then we all realized that he was the one who had told the Attolians about the trail up the mountain."

I remembered the fancy tortoiseshell comb of Ambiades's that had caught the magus's eye. He must have wondered where Ambiades got the money to afford it. I'd guessed that Ambiades was in somebody's pay and that from time to time he felt guilty about it, but I'd assumed he was taking money from an enemy of the magus's in Sounis's court. It hadn't occurred to me, or to the magus, obviously, that he could betray his master to the Attolians.

"Ambiades started to say something, but then you screamed."

I screamed?

"We could hear you from the top of the cliff when they pulled the sword out," Sophos told me, his voice shaking—and I remembered. That was the muddled and awful part. I'd felt my life dragged out with the sword, but in the end my life wouldn't go. It had stretched between me and the sword. I think that only the power of the gods could have kept me alive, but my living was at the same time an offense to them. I should have died, but instead the pain went on and on. Dying would have been so much easier.

I shuddered, and the pain returned, stopping my breath. Sophos held me by the hand until it passed.

"Everyone looked down at you," he said. "Then we turned to look at Ambiades, and he didn't care. I mean, we could see that he didn't care that you were dead. I don't think that he cared about anything anymore, not about me or the magus or Pol. And Pol, he just put out one hand and shoved Ambiades over the edge. And then—"

Sophos stopped for another deep breath before he went on. "Then he went over the cliff, too, with two of the Attolians. The magus tried to get out his sword, but the soldiers knocked him down."

Sophos pulled his knees up to his chest and rocked back and forth as he cried.

Moving slowly, I lifted one hand to his leg to squeeze it. I couldn't think of anything to say. I had liked Pol.

"I've known Pol my entire life," Sophos said unevenly. "I don't *want* him to be dead," he insisted, as if his wishes should be granted. "He has a wife, and he has two children," he wailed, "and I am going to have to tell them."

I shuddered and closed my eyes again. The man I'd killed could have had no clue that he was facing a skilled opponent. He'd judged me by my novice sword and my size. I had taken him by surprise and killed him. I might just as well have stabbed him in the back in an alley. Did he have a wife and two children? Who would tell them that he was dead? The pain in my chest spread, until even my fingers ached, where the backs of them touched the rough floor.

After a long time Sophos whispered, "Gen? Are you still awake?"

"Yes."

"The magus said that the bleeding stopped and that you would probably be all right. As long as you didn't get a fever."

"That's good to know." That way they could behead me.

The sun was setting when the guards brought the magus back. Its last light came directly in the small window and lit the opposite wall of the cell. The wall was made of the same yellow limestone as the king's megaron on the other side of the Eddis mountains. I'd dozed on and off during the afternoon. Someone had brought food, which I'd told Sophos to eat.

"Gen, how do you feel?" the magus asked.

"Oh, fine," I told him. My chest was filled with boiling cement, and I was hot and cold all over at the same time, but I didn't really care. I didn't care much about anything, so I guess I felt fine.

The magus held his hand against my forehead and looked concerned. "Did you eat anything today?"

I rolled my eyes.

"Yes," he agreed, "that was a silly question. Did you get anything to eat, Sophos?"

Sophos nodded.

"Did you save anything for me?"

"No, I'm sorry." Sophos looked guilty.

"That's all right," lied the magus. "I ate upstairs, while I was talking with the captain of the Queen's Guard. Evidently Her Majesty is on her way to hear our story for herself."

He settled himself on the stone floor and leaned against the wall, just outside my line of sight.

"We are in a slightly difficult position," he said, and I rolled my eyes again. "I'm afraid that Ambiades was our only reliable means of convincing the Attolians that Hamiathes's Gift was lost. You know what happened to Ambiades?"

"Sophos told me." It was awkward to have a conversation directed to the side of my head, but turning to look at the magus wasn't worth the effort.

"His father's money must have run out, and he decided he'd rather be a wealthy traitor than an impoverished apprentice. Attolia paid him, and he had arranged for someone to follow us from the time we left the king's city in Sounis. If we moved too quickly, Ambiades was careful to slow us down." We both thought of the food missing from the saddlebags.

"I owe you many apologies," the magus admitted.

"They are all accepted," I said. It wasn't important anymore.

"The queen probably hoped to kill the rest of us quietly and send Ambiades back as a sole survivor. She is not going to be happy to have lost such a valuable spy, and with Ambiades dead, I'm afraid there's no way to convince her that Hamiathes's Gift fell in a stream."

There was a pause while each of us considered the Attolians' means of extracting reliable information.

The magus changed the subject, and I swiveled my head to look at him when he said, "Attolia's soldiers have been to the temple in the dystopia." He nodded. I'm not sure if he meant to affirm the truth of what he'd said or if he was pleased to have elicited a sign of life from me at last. "The temple was completely destroyed. The Aracthus had broken through the roof and washed away most of the walls. There were still signs that there had been some sort of man-made construction at the site, but that was all."

"When?"

"I can't be sure, but no more than a day or two after we left."

I remembered how close the water of the Aracthus had sounded as it washed over the roof of the gods' hall. I thought of it pouring down into the room and the maze below, washing out the doors and walls. I thought of the gods in their beautiful robes and Hephestia on her throne, gone. I turned my head back toward the ceiling of the cell and blinked water out of my eyes. The magus sensed my distress and lifted himself across the floor to console me.

"Gen, it was an old temple. The collapse of the main door was probably the first sign of the damage caused when the Aracthus forced its way through a new entrance somewhere. In the next few days the power of the water destroyed the temple entirely. It would have happened sooner or later. All the things man has made are eventually destroyed." He stopped a tear as it rolled down toward my ear. "I wish, though, that I had gone in with you," he said. "I'll always wonder what you saw." He waited a moment, hoping that I might say something.

"Won't tell me or can't?" he asked.

"Can't," I admitted. "Not that I would anyway." I goaded him.

He laughed, then checked my forehead again for fever.

A guard brought more food. The magus and Sophos ate. The square of yellow sunlight on the wall opposite the window had dimmed when we heard more footsteps in the corridor and knew that the queen must have arrived at the castle and sent for the magus.

"I'll do what I can for you, Gen," the magus promised as he stood up. They took Sophos as well, and I was left alone in the cell, wondering what the magus thought he could possibly do for me.

\*   \*   \*

The cell was pitch-dark when he returned. The guards carried lanterns, and I closed my eyes against their glare, assuming that they would be gone soon. When someone nudged me with his boot, I groaned a little, partly because it hurt, partly because I was offended that they were bothering me. Another fiercer nudge dug into my ribs, and I opened my eyes. Standing over me, between the magus and the captain of the guard, was the queen of Attolia.

She smiled at my surprise. Standing in the light, surrounded by the dark beyond the reach of the lanterns, she seemed lit by the aura of the gods. Her hair was black and held away from her face by an imitation of the woven gold band of Hephestia. Her robe was draped like a peplos, made from embroidered red velvet. She was as tall as the magus, and she was more beautiful than any woman I have ever seen. Everything about her brought to mind the old religion, and I knew that the resemblance was deliberate, intended to remind her subjects that as Hephestia ruled uncontested among the gods, this woman ruled Attolia. Too bad that I had seen the Great Goddess and knew how far the Attolian queen fell short of her mark.

She spoke, and her voice was quiet and lovely. "The magus of Sounis informs me that you are a thief of unsurpassed skills." She smiled gently.

"I am," I answered, truthfully.

"He suggests, however, that your loyalty to your own country is not strong."

I winced. "I have no particular loyalty to the king of Sounis, Your Majesty."

"How fortunate for you. I don't believe he holds you in high regard."

"No, Your Majesty. He probably doesn't."

She smiled again. Her perfect teeth showed. "Then there's

nothing to prevent you from remaining in Attolia to be *my* thief."
I looked over at the magus. This was the favor he had done me:
convinced the queen that I was too valuable to throw away.

"Uh," I said, "there is one thing, Your Majesty."

The queen's eyebrows rose in delicate arches of astonishment.
"What would that be?"

I had to think of something quickly. Discretion prevented me
from saying that I thought she was a fiend from the underworld
and that mountain lions couldn't force me to enter her service.
As I searched for something safer to say, I remembered the
magus's comment on the banks of the Aracthus. "I have a sweetheart," I said with complete conviction. "Your Majesty, I've
promised to return to her."

The queen was amused. The magus was consternated. He
couldn't guess why I would throw away a chance to save myself.
There were certainly no love affairs written up in my record at
the king's prison. I was sure because I had written the record
myself. It had been an easy way to turn a lot of boasting into a
solid reputation, and it hadn't been difficult to slip it in among
the real records. Anyone who can steal the king's seal ring can
manage the locks on his record room.

"You are promised to someone?" said the queen, in disbelief.

"I am, Your Majesty," I said firmly.

"And you will not break your promise?" She shook her head
sadly.

"I couldn't, Your Majesty."

"Surely I am a better mistress to serve?"

"You are more beautiful, Your Majesty." The queen smiled
again before I finished. "But she is more kind."

So much for discretion. The smile disappeared. You could
have heard a pin drop onto the stone floor as her alabaster cheeks
flushed red. No one could ever accuse the queen of Attolia of
being kind.

She smiled again at me, a different, thinner smile, and inclined her head in acceptance of a point scored. I smiled back, pleased with myself in a bitter way, until she turned to the captain of her guard.

"Take him upstairs and fetch a doctor," she ordered. "We will give him an opportunity to change his mind." Her red peplos swept across the back of my hand as she turned to leave, and I winced. The velvet was soft, but the embroidery scratched.

In a room several floors above the dungeon, I lay in bed while my fever climbed. I raved, and in a distant way I knew that I was raving. Moira came to sit by my bed. She assured me that I wasn't dying. I told her that I wished I were. Then Eugenides came out of the dark, and Moira was gone. Eugenides was patient at first. He reminded me that lives are things to be stolen sometimes, just like any possession. He asked me if I would prefer to be dead myself. I said I would, and he asked what then would have become of my plans for fame and my name carved in stone. And would I then leave my companions to die as well?

I didn't like to think of the magus as a companion. But if he wasn't, why had I risked my life once for him already? I sighed. And then there was Sophos to worry over as well. I said that if only I could have died when the soldier pulled the sword out, I wouldn't be bothered by my conscience. The god beside me was silent, and the silence stretched out from my bedside through the castle and, it seemed, throughout the world as I remembered that Lyopidus had burned and died while Eugenides had not.

After countless empty heartbeats, Eugenides spoke again from a distance. "His wife died in the winter. His three children live with their aunt in Eia."

When I dared to lower my arm, he was gone. I slept again, and when I woke, I was more clearheaded. Leaving Sophos and the magus to certain death wouldn't do anything for my conscience, even if I died myself soon after. And there was fame and fortune to consider. I dragged myself out of bed and started to look around the room.

The bolts in the door of the cell turned over and the door swung open. The lamps in the hallway weren't burning, and neither the magus nor Sophos could see who stood in the doorway.

"It's me," I hissed, before they could make a noise that might carry to the guardroom. I heard them moving toward my voice and backed away so that they wouldn't bump into me. Once they were in the passage, I asked Sophos if he still had his overshirt on.

"Why?"

"I want you to give it to me."

"Why?"

"Because all I'm wearing is bandages. They took my clothes." Sophos pulled the shirt off and held it out in my direction, nearly poking me in the eye.

"Do you want my shoes, too?" he offered.

"No, I'm better off barefoot."

"Gen," said the magus, "you shouldn't do this."

"Get dressed?"

"You know what I mean." At least he had the sense to whisper. "I thank you for opening the door, but the best thing you can do now is forget all about us. Climb back up where you came from and pretend you never left your bed."

"And how will you get yourselves the rest of the way out of here? Through the front door?"

"We'll manage."

I snorted very quietly. "You will not."

"If we're caught, we can claim that we bribed a guard."

I dismissed him with a wave of my hand, which he couldn't

see. "We should get moving," I said, making herding motions with my good hand, which he also couldn't see.

"Gen, it's only been two days. Three since we were arrested. You can't manage."

"I think," I said stiffly, "that I am more of an asset than a liability."

"Gen, that's not what I meant." He put out one hand in the dark to touch my shoulder, but I shifted away. "Gen, we can't ask you to risk yourself again."

"This is a change from your earlier position," I pointed out.

"I was wrong before."

"You're wrong now, too."

"Gen, the queen of Attolia doesn't bear you any ill will."

I thought about her parting smile. "I think she does," I said.

"All she wants from you is a promise of your service."

"Well, she isn't going to get it." I'd heard too many stories about the things that happened to people who worked for her. "Can we stop discussing this just now?" I started to move away as I spoke, and they followed me in the darkness. With my feet bare, I stepped gingerly, and it was easy to remember to favor my bad shoulder.

"How did you get the keys? Where are the guards?" Sophos wouldn't stop talking as we moved through the pitch-dark. "And why are all the lanterns out?"

I sighed. "I didn't get the keys. They took my clothes and probably burnt them. They left my lock openers and the other things from my pockets on a table in my room." I'd left the magus's cloak pin and Ambiades's comb behind. I'd brought the penknife in case I needed it again. We came to a corner, and I felt my way around it, then reached back to take Sophos by the hand.

"Be quiet," I whispered, "and try not to pull on me." I was a little unsteady on my feet and afraid that he would pull me right over if he stumbled.

"What about the guards," he persisted, "and the lanterns?"

The guards, I told him, were at the end of the corridor guarding a deck of cards, and the lanterns were out because I blew them out. "This way," I hissed, "when they hear us chatting like happy sparrows in our nest, they won't *immediately* be able to find us."

"But where are we going?"

"Would you shut up?"

My left hand, the bad one, brushed along the wall until it bumped against a door handle. The pain stopped me in my tracks, and I squeezed Sophos's hand hard to prevent him from bumping me. "Hold on," I whispered. They stood quietly while I worked the lock on the door. Fortunately I had a key that fit closely enough and could turn it with one hand. "Watch the door," I said as I pulled it open. It rumbled, but the hinges didn't squeak. "Don't bang your head," I warned the magus.

We walked down a tunnel only as wide as the door. The walls arched into the ceiling just a few inches over my head. There was a stone door at the end that had a simple crossbar fastening on the inside. Once through it, we were outside the castle on a narrow footing of stone that ran under its walls. In the silence we could hear waves lapping against the stone under our feet, and in the river there were ghosts of reflections from torches set in sconces along the sentry walk above our heads.

"What is this?" Sophos asked.

"It's the Seperchia," said the magus. "Remember this stronghold sits in the middle of the river and defends the bridge to either side."

"I meant, what is this?" Sophos said, and stamped his foot on the stone under him.

"This is a ledge that runs around the entire castle," I explained, "so that they can maintain the foundation. We're going to follow it to the bridge into town. Keep your voices down. There are guards."

"Why is there a door?"

I left it to the magus to answer.

"They dispose of bodies by throwing them in the river."

"Oh."

"Sometimes the guards will sell a body back to the family if they wait here in a boat," he said.

Sophos finally kept his mouth shut as we crabbed our way around the castle. There was no moon. I couldn't see my hand in front of my face, so I kept it on the castle wall and checked with my forward foot to make sure there was always ground underneath me. The magus put himself between me and Sophos, and he was careful not to bump. We crept around one corner, and then another. There were no torches burning on the bridge, and if there were guards watching, they were posted on the towers, not on the bridge itself. The three of us snuck across.

Getting through town proved to be trickier than leaving the castle. Without the moon we had to pick our way carefully, and I had a difficult time leading the way I wanted to go. The fires in the houses had been banked hours ago, and there was no glow through the windows to help us. Dogs barked as we passed, but no watch came to check on them. The road from the castle led away from the river. We left it, hoping to cut back to the water, and got lost in narrow streets. Twice I almost walked headlong into the invisible walls of houses before we finally came to another road that ran along the riverbank and passed a bridge.

"We stay on this side," I said, and the magus didn't argue. We moved very slowly past dark houses. I was happier without moonlight because I didn't have to worry about hiding, and going slowly, I had time as I took each step to favor my shoulder.

"Gen," the magus asked, "how are you?"

"Good enough." I answered, a little surprised at how capable I was feeling. I was weak but clearheaded. My shoulder hurt, but in a distant way. The pain was only sharp when I stumbled, and I didn't stumble often. I felt as if I were floating very gently down the road, buoyed by an invisible cloud. The night all around was filled with the usual noise of bugs and jumping fish and distant dogs howling, but there seemed to be a bubble of silence that surrounded us.

The moon eventually came up, and the going was easier, but the magus didn't try to hurry me. He and Sophos were both patient, but Sophos kept wanting to chatter as we walked. I realized that he was frightened and that talking helped him, but I needed to concentrate all my energy on my feet. The magus talked with him. We kept moving until just before dawn.

We weren't many miles from town, but the road we followed ran up against a rise and turned inland. In order to stay with the river, we needed to follow a narrower path that climbed through the rocks along the bank. We stopped to rest. I leaned against a convenient stone pile and slid to the ground. I tucked Sophos's overshirt, which was fortunately a long one, underneath me and closed my eyes. My feet were cold. I ignored them and slept for a while. When I opened my eyes again, there was enough light to see the color of the world. The magus's overshirt was wrapped around my feet, and the magus was gone.

I jerked my head around to look for him, and wished I hadn't. My body had stiffened while I slept. Sophos was still asleep beside me, curled up on the ground. The magus was standing a little way away, looking down through the rocks at the river. I called him, and when he turned to look at me, his face was bleak. Little birds began to peck in my stomach.

"What's the matter?" I asked him.

"The river is running the wrong way."

Let the gods into your life and you rapidly lose faith in the natural laws. The little birds stopped pecking, and they all fell over dead. I had a stomach full of dead birds for a moment as I thought that he meant the river had truly reversed its direction. He only meant that he had been mistaken during the night about which way it was flowing.

The magus sat down and put his head in his hands. "I lost my sense of direction in the town," he said. "We haven't been following the river downstream toward the pass. We've been going upstream. The ground was rising gradually, but I didn't notice until we reached this steeper part. I have no idea where we are."

Sophos sat up blinking just then, so no one noticed my sigh of relief. "What's the matter?" he asked, looking at the magus, who explained. All he knew was that we were on the far side of the dystopia from the Sea of Olives. That was why the road we were following had turned. Upriver there was no more arable land. There was no way of knowing how far the track we were on might lead us up the river. The ground would rise and get rockier and more difficult to cover. As far as the magus knew, there might be no bridges at all before the dystopia ran into the foot of the mountains, where we would be trapped.

"There's a trade route on the far side of the river, and I'm sure there are some villages, but I don't know why any of them would want a bridge to the dystopia."

"What about this road we've been on?" I asked, although I knew the answer.

"It's been getting narrower," the magus said, "and beyond here it turns into a track and probably dead-ends at the next farm. I went to look."

"So what do we do?" Sophos asked the magus.

"We keep going," I said. "We can't go back without running into a search party." I rested my head against the stone for another moment. "We'll stick to the river and hope that there are enough rocks to slow down any horses. There's no reason for us to have gone this way, and they'll probably concentrate their searching in the other direction."

"We could hide in the dystopia for a while," suggested Sophos. "We could cross it and go back through the Sea of Olives."

The magus looked sideways at me. "We couldn't get across the Aracthus."

"We could wait until Gen is better."

"What about food?"

Not being at all hungry, I had forgotten about food. "At least we have plenty of water," I said optimistically, and started to get up. I felt like one of the damaged clocks that my brother sometimes worked on. The magus bent down to give me a hand. Sophos turned to help as well.

"Do you really think that they'll search for us? Won't be-heading us start a war?" he asked.

I considered the prestige value of cutting the head off one of your enemy's premier advisors and compared it to the drawbacks of an all-out war. "She might let you two go"—I nodded—"to avoid a war or to delay one until she's ready."

"What about you?" Sophos asked.

"She might let me go as well. But she'd probably like best to catch me and let you two slip away." No one was going to start a war over me, and I could be tremendously useful if I could be induced to work for her. I shivered, and something that wanted to be a groan came out of my mouth as a sigh. We had to stay close to the river because if we were going to be caught, I planned to throw myself in.

Once I was on my feet, momentum carried me forward. We followed a goat track that ran across the rocks right beside the river. The crumbled stones on the path rubbed the skin off the bottom of my feet, but I could see better, and we moved a little faster than before.

As we walked, mostly single file, Sophos continued to talk. "Gen?" he asked. "If you could be anywhere you wanted right now, where would it be?"

I sighed. "In bed," I said. "In a big bed, with a carved footboard, in a warm room with a lot of windows. And sheets," I added after I'd taken a few more steps, thinking of them rubbing against my sore feet, "as nice as the ones they sell on the Sacred Way. And a fireplace," I added, expanding the daydream. "And books."

"Books?" he asked, surprised.

"Books," I said firmly, not caring if the magus thought it was odd. "Lots of books. Where would you be?"

"Under the apricot tree in my mother's garden at the villa. I'd be watching my little sisters play, and anytime I wanted one, I'd reach up and pick another apricot."

"They aren't ripe this time of year."

"Well, say you can be any place any time you like. Where would you be, magus?"

The magus was quiet so long that I thought he wasn't going to answer.

"I'd be in the main temple," he said at last.

"Urgh," I said, still associating the temple with boredom—a lot of people chanting and incense everywhere. My new, vehement belief in the gods had made me no more tolerant of the empty mumbling I'd seen in temples all my life.

The magus wasn't finished. "Watching the marriage of Sounis and Eddis."

I made a face. "Why are you so keen on this marriage?"

"The king needs an heir, and that heir needs to inherit Eddis as well as Sounis."

"He does have a nephew," Sophos pointed out.

"I'm sorry, of course he has an heir," said the magus. "But he needs a son of his own for the throne to be secure. Which means he needs to have a wife."

"And why should his heir be entitled to Eddis?" I asked.

He thought I deserved a complete answer, which shows more than anything how much his opinion of me had changed. "Entitled not just to Eddis but to Attolia as well," he said. "You would have no way of knowing, Gen, but these three countries are free only by a rare combination of circumstances. The earliest invaders overran our country because they wanted us to pay them tribute. They were slowly replaced by the Merchant Empire, which mostly wanted our trade, and those overlords we eventually drove away. We could do that only because the Merchant Empire was busy fighting a greater threat elsewhere, the Medes. The Medes have been trying for a hundred years to expand their empire to span the middle sea. Soon they will want not only our land but to drive us off of it. For years and years they have fought what remains of the Merchant Empire, and while they fight, we are free. But when they are done fighting, Sounis, Eddis, and Attolia must be united to fight the winner or we will be subjugated as we never were before. There will be no Sounis, no Attolia, no Eddis, only Mede."

"You're sure the Medes will win?"

"I'm sure."

It was something to think about while we trudged along. We were rising above the river; the bank grew steeper until it was dropping straight down six or eight feet into the water. We walked on a narrow trail of dirt packed on top of stones. To the left of the trail the stones were piled even higher. The river was narrower and deeper the further we went upstream. I could hear it churning as it forced its way through its narrow channel. The opposite bank was only a few hundred yards away, and once we passed a tiny, empty village. There were no trees, and the sun grew hotter. On our left the stones rose higher, cutting off our line of sight at every twist in the path.

When we came to another rise in the path, the magus helped Sophos climb onto a rock to look downriver.

"Do you see anyone?" we both asked him.

He said no and began to scramble down.

"Wait," I said. "Do you see any dust?"

"You mean, in the air? Yes, there's a cloud."

"That's horses on the road," I said to the magus.

He agreed as he helped Sophos down. We tried to hurry, but while I wasn't in much pain, I didn't have the strength to move any faster. The next time Sophos looked he could see a glimpse of the horses as they came single file between the rocks. We walked on, until I caught my foot on a stone and stumbled forward. The magus was ahead of me. He heard me catch my breath and turned to help, but by that time I'd hit the ground. He tried to help me up but reached for the wrong shoulder. I could only flutter a hand in distress. My grandfather would have been proud of his training. A thief never makes a noise by accident. I bit my lip.

"Gen? Gen, don't faint. We'll leave the path and try to hide somewhere in the rocks. They may go past."

"No," I said. That was a hopeless plan, and we both knew it. If he and Sophos left me, they might get away, but there was a better alternative. Between breaths, I said, "There's a bridge." Upriver, islands of rock divided the flow of water. Debris had been swept down the river when it was in flood and had lodged against the rocks. One tree trunk stretched from our bank to a pile of rock in the center of the river.

The magus looked over his shoulder and saw the makeshift bridge. "Do you think we can get across?"

"Yes." There was a second collection of branches that crossed to the far bank. It was more fragile, but it would bear my weight and probably the magus's.

The bridge, such as it was, was still several hundred yards away. The horsemen were only twice that distance behind us. It was a race between the tortoise and the hare, but the tortoise had just enough head start, and he had the magus to drag him along. We reached the makeshift crossing with the pursuers just behind. They'd left their horses. They couldn't manage the many pitfalls in the trail, and the men moved faster on foot.

"Sophos, you go first," said the magus. "Then I'll help Gen across."

"No," I said.

"Should I try to walk?" asked Sophos.

"No!" I insisted that he get on his hands and knees and creep across. One slip and he would be sucked into the river and probably never seen again. A river runs fastest at its narrowest point, and all of the water of the Seperchia had to squeeze between these banks. It was deceptively smooth, but it had the strength to drag a man under in a heartbeat. Sophos safely crawled to the island in the center of the river.

"We'll go together, Gen," the magus said.

"No."

"Gen, I won't leave you again."

He looked over my shoulder at the men coming behind and tried to pull my good hand. By then I think he was fairly sure that the guards would let him and Sophos slip away.

"Gen—"

"You have to tell Sophos that if the branches on the second bridge sag underneath him, he has to jump to the riverbank. If he tries to cross with his feet in the water, he'll drown."

The magus checked on Sophos, who was beginning to cross the second, more fragile bridge. It was made of small tree branches bundled together by the water and held in place where those branches had caught in crevices between the rocks. The wood was brittle, and as branches broke, the bridge dropped closer to the water. The magus knew Archimedes's principle as well as I did.

"Gen?" He turned back to me.

"I can manage. I promise," I told him.

Reluctantly he went. He crawled as carefully as Sophos.

Once he reached the island, I slithered down the bank to where the tree trunk was lodged and walked across. The wood had been washed smooth by the water and was a comfort to my bare feet. If it had been half as wide, I would have had no trouble.

The magus grinned as I landed on the rocks beside him and I turned to give him what help I could dislodging the bridge. There was a man starting to cross, but he jumped back to safety before the log came free. The current sucked it away. Over the drumming of water we could hear cursing.

I sent the magus across the second bridge. He went without protest; then I started across. Many of the small branches that held the bridge in place had broken under the magus's weight, and it sagged dangerously near the water. If it dropped any lower, it would be swept away by the current, but the branches that had held the magus's weight held mine as well. Halfway across, I saw the length of rope, twisted in the branches. I crept through the tangle of branches onto the rocks beside the magus, just as the men behind me began firing their handheld guns. I wasn't very worried. The new guns will stop an infantry charge, but they can't be aimed well enough to allow the rifleman to pick his target. Crossbows would have been much more dangerous, but the queen of Attolia liked to have her personal guard carry the rifles because she thought they were more impressive.

I pointed out the rope to the magus and asked if he could reach it. I had to shout above the sound of the river.

"They might be able to find another tree trunk on their bank. It would be better to get rid of both bridges."

The magus nodded his head and grabbed on to a rock as he swung out over the river. He picked free a strand of the frayed rope and pulled on it. It broke in his hand. The men on the opposite bank fired again. The magus moved more slowly and picked three or four of the rope ends out of the tangle of the branches before he pulled. This time they held, and the whole bridge twitched and bent. The brittle branches broke off, the bridge shortened a few inches, and the far end dropped into the water. The current swept everything away.

Just then a bullet hit the rock near the magus's hand. His hand slipped, and he fell forward with his left arm and shoulder in the river. He managed to keep his head up, but even so, the Seperchia nearly dragged him down. Sophos and I both grabbed him by the waistband, Sophos with both hands, I with only one. We pulled with all our strength. The magus kicked his feet, looking for a foothold and, with our help, backed himself out of the water. The riflemen fired again as we all sank behind large rocks, out of their sight. We picked our way between the rocks, up the steep bank of the river. It rose steeply about ten feet, and then the ground dropped away a little. We were safe from any more stray bullets, and we stopped to rest. Only then did I notice the blood dripping down my shirtfront. I touched my fingers gingerly to my check.

"One of the bullets must have knocked loose a shard of rock," the magus said. "It's taken a divot out of your face, I'm afraid."

"All my beauty gone." I sighed.

"It might heal clean," the magus reassured me, although he could see that I was joking.

"I don't think so," I said, feeling the shape of the hole in the skin with my finger. I was quite certain I'd have a feather-shaped white scar. Getting across the makeshift bridge had been well done, and the god of thieves agreed, although some might not recognize his sign of approval.

"What if they sent a party up this side of the river as well?" Sophos asked.

The magus looked at me, and I shrugged with one shoulder. "We can look," I said. We had left the dystopia behind on the far side of the river. There were rocks along the bank on this side, but the ground quickly flattened out into rolling fields broken by lines of scrub and trees. A road ran between the fields and the river. There were no houses as far as we could see, and no sign of anyone on the road.

"I think we can hope for the best," I said. "But those men might ride back downstream, cross the bridge, and come up this side. We should keep moving."

"Moving where?" the magus asked.

I shrugged again and waved my good hand upriver. "That way." Away from the people who might be pursuing us.

We slid down the bank to the road and walked up it. The road was a cart track of powdered dirt. My feet were happier, and with fewer jolts my shoulder was happier as well. The reassuring sensation of floating down the road returned. As we walked, the fields on our right disappeared and were replaced with land that had been cleared once but not farmed for a long time. Wild grasses grew, and there were bushes, but we were the tallest thing in the landscape. I felt very exposed.

I felt much better when the sun dropped behind the hills and night fell, but then the cold came. A half hour after the sun was gone, a chill wind blew down the back of my neck. The magus and Sophos didn't seem bothered by it. I pushed myself a little faster to warm up and breathed with my mouth open to keep my teeth from chattering. I couldn't dismiss the crawling sensation in the middle of my back. I was thinking that the Attolian queen wanted at least one of her prisoners back very badly.

The mountains were ahead of us, and we continued toward them in the dark. On this side of the range they rose very steeply, directly out of the Attolian plain, just as they had risen out of the Sea of Olives. We kept to the road by feel. When my bare feet stepped into the stubble, I knew that we had wandered from the track. Even with the breeze pushing me down the road, we walked very slowly. I was tired. I could still hear the roar of the river in its chasm, and I longed for a drink of clean water. When I began to stumble, the magus took my arm, but he was too tall. Sophos slipped under my good shoulder and supported me. Thoughts of the riders that might be behind kept us moving.

After a long time the moon rose, and the Seperchia, which had curved away from the road, began to curve back. The ground we were on had been rising, and the river ran beside us through a chasm thirty or forty feet deep. Its far bank was a cliff face that lifted straight up to the shoulders of the mountains. If we hadn't crossed at the makeshift bridge, the trail we had been following would have dumped us into the water.

Our road ended in a bridge, and without discussion we started across it. Just before we reached the top of its stone arch, the magus stopped and then turned around. If he'd had ears like a horse, he would have swiveled them forward.

"What do you hear?" I asked.

"Hoofbeats."

We crossed over the bridge and walked directly into the arms of the soldiers waiting there.

# chapter 12

_T_HERE WAS A ledge on the far side of the bridge. At the back of it a squat tower defended a gate that closed off a cleft in the cliff face. The gate was open, and soldiers were scattered around three different fires in front of it, playing dice, sleeping, doing whatever soldiers do when they are off duty. There were only two guards posted at the bridge, and they were sitting on the stone pilings at the end. They didn't see us until we arrived almost at their feet, and for a moment all they could do was stare. Then they smirked. Then they both jumped down, and one planted his spear beside us, looking suddenly crisp and military while the other guard ran to find his captain. No one said a word while we waited. Around the fires the soldiers didn't even look up from their dice games.

When the captain arrived, he didn't have much more to say

than his guards. While he looked us over, I leaned on Sophos, and the magus supported us both.

The captain shook his head. To the magus he said, "Welcome to Eddis." Then he turned to his lieutenant, who had come up behind him. "Get horses," he said succinctly. "And four or five guards to take them. This is not for us to figure out. Get up on the bridge where you belong," he said to the two guards, and they scrambled to the top of the arched bridge and looked out over the moonlit plain from there. "You three can follow me," he said to us, crooking a finger in our direction.

A few soldiers in the camp noticed the movement by the bridge, and heads began to turn. The signs of relaxation disappeared, and the soldiers suddenly became professionals, eager and suspicious. By the time the lieutenant returned with five men and six small horses, the hoofbeats that the magus had heard had been heard by the guards as well and reported to the captain.

"That will be the Attolian guard," said the magus. He might have expected to be handed over right then.

"I'll deal with them," the captain said to the lieutenant. "You take care of these." He waved a disgusted hand in our direction. Then, signaling to more of his guards to attend him, he tramped away.

Horses were mounted with a lot of jingling and thumping, and a beefy soldier tugged Sophos out from under my arm. Taking him by the elbow and the seat of the pants, he swung him onto a horse. Somebody took my elbow, intending to do the same thing, but as they tugged, I swiveled around and sagged to my knees.

"Stop! Don't do that!" shouted Sophos, his voice breaking, as he struggled to get down from the horse. The beefy soldier held him pinned and told him to calm down.

The man holding my arm looked a little closer at my face and suggested someone get a blanket. The one they fetched was warm from lying next to the fire. They wrapped me in it and then lifted me up gently into the lieutenant's arms.

As the horses crossed under the gate, I saw carved griffons overhead, and then I think I fell asleep. I dreamt of rock walls moving past on either side and heard in my sleep the crashing of the ponies' hooves as they climbed the stone roadway that ran up the cleft in the mountains, cut by the Aracthus before its path had changed.

When we reached the palace, the main courtyard was lit by lanterns, but most of the windows were dark. It was long past midnight. Everyone climbed off his horse, and two men helped me to the ground. After that there was a lot of hemming and hawing, and no one really knew what to do. Sophos came and tucked himself under my good shoulder. The magus stood beside us. All the others sidled a little farther away as if they were afraid our troubles might be contagious.

Finally someone opened the double doors that led to the entrance hall, and we trooped in. The clatter of boots on the marble floors announced our arrival to anyone who hadn't heard the noise in the courtyard. Servants and onlookers appeared at the heads of the two staircases. Lights were still burning in the lesser throne room, and the great knot of us moved in that direction. The people on the stairs were sucked down in our wake, and by the time we'd left the dark entrance hall and crowded into the doorway of the brightly lit throne room, I felt like the center of a circus on the move. All we needed was dancing bears.

At first all I could see of the room was the walls near the ceiling where mountain swallows were painted swooping and diving, but a series of stairs led into the room, and as the people ahead of me stepped down, I could see where the lower walls were stained dark red and two gold griffons lay, one on either side of the throne. The throne was empty. At the raised hearth in front of it a group of women had been sitting and talking, and two of them had been playing chess. By far the least attractive of the women stood up.

She had black hair, like Attolia, and her gown was red velvet, but there all similarities between her and the lowland queen ended. The queen of Eddis tended to stand like a soldier. The ruffles on her shoulders made her arms seem long enough to reach to her knees. Her nose had been broken and had reknitted crooked; her hair was cut short like a man's and curled so much over her simple silver crown that the crown itself was nearly invisible.

She located the lieutenant who'd brought us and demanded an explanation of him. Unable to hear her over the babbling of so many people, he shrugged apologetically.

She raised one hand and quirked an eyebrow at the crowd. The room fell quiet. The soldiers around the magus, Sophos, and me stepped hastily aside. Once the queen saw us, she dropped her hand.

"Oh," she said in irritation and perfect understanding. "It's you, Eugenides."

I looked down at my dust-covered feet. I was tired, and I felt as light as a cloud that might blow away across the sky at any moment. I didn't even have the strength to feel chagrin at embarrassing my queen and staunchest defender once again by providing a spectacle for the entire court of Eddis. I'd never been so happy to hear my own name.

The magus, I noted, was not surprised by the greeting. I was a little annoyed because I had wanted to see his jaw drop. I had to satisfy myself with Sophos's surprise—he was gaping in a heartwarming way—and hope that the magus didn't know all my secrets.

"Down the steps," I whispered in Sophos's ear, as I nudged

him forward. While he helped me, the people on either side moved even farther away, not sure whether the queen's irritation might spill over to them. They needn't have worried. I had disappeared months before without her approval, but she and a few of her ministers must have guessed why, and if she was angry at me, it was only because she'd been worrying.

With my good hand I reached under the braid at the base of my neck to free the thong that was tied there. It was the shorter of the two that Pol had given me on the banks of the Aracthus. One-handed, I couldn't easily get the knot undone, and several strands of my own dark hair came with the thong when I pulled it free.

I glanced back briefly at the magus and was delighted to see his mouth open in astonishment.

"Gen," he said under his breath, "you viper."

Above the queen's extended palm I held Hamiathes's Gift. It had hung hidden by my hair since I'd braided it there after the first fighting in the Sea of Olives. As soon as I'd seen the riders attacking, I'd moved my horse, never far away from the magus's, until I could cut the thong around his neck with the penknife I'd stolen the first or second day out of prison. He'd been too distracted to notice and had assumed later, as I'd known he would, that the thong had been sliced by a sword stroke and that the Gift had dropped into the stream.

It swung from its leather loop for a moment, such a little boring river stone, but no one in the room doubted its authenticity. The precisely cut runes of Hephestia's mark swung first toward me and then away. The sapphire hidden in the stone caught the light, and the carved letters seemed to hover, bright blue, in the air.

I had a speech to make. I'd worked it up on the way down the mountain to Sounis and practiced it over and over in the king's prison, but I couldn't remember any of it, and besides, I was too tired. That I carried Hamiathes's Gift to my queen was all that had kept me going from the Attolian stronghold to the top of the mountains. The moment I released the stone, darkness rushed in, and I leaned toward the floor without saying anything.

I slept for a long time untroubled by visions of the gods, and when I woke, I was in my own bed. I brushed my hand back and forth across the soft sheets. They were as fine as anything sold in Sounis because all of Sounis's best linens were woven in Eddis. At my feet the footboard was carved with a scene of fir trees against the skyline of the sacred mountains, and when I turned my head, I could see the sacred mountains themselves through the windows. They rose up in all directions, safely hemming me in.

I remembered the story that said Hephestia had made the valleys in the mountains for her chosen people, and I wondered if it was true. Having seen the gods, I continued to doubt all of the stories I had heard about them. If the gods were incarnations of the mountains and rivers around us, or whether they drew their power from those sources, I couldn't say. They had power greater than any mortal, and if that power was enough to change the face of the earth, I didn't want to know. I only hoped that they would hear my prayers from a distance, accept my offerings, and not trouble my dreams again. Hamiathes's Gift was more burden than blessing, and I was glad to be free of it.

I lay and admired the view for a while before I realized that there were people talking quietly in the library, which was separated by an open doorway from the room that was both my bedroom and study. I turned my head to listen better. The magus was talking with the queen. I heard him address someone as Minister and thought that probably meant minister of war.

"We deliberately made the king's message to you as vague as possible, so Gen may have hoped to find the stone in our possession. When he couldn't find it or any reference to it in my papers, I believe he decided to make a reputation for himself, not just as a thief but as a Sounisian one. He mentioned an Eddisian mother in the forged court records to explain his dark coloring and any trace of an accent that he couldn't hide, and then he bragged about his ability to perform some outstanding feat that would have to come to my attention. He could only have hoped that it would occur to me that I needed a proficient but anonymous thief whose absence from the city wouldn't be noticed. He couldn't have known that the man he bragged to in the wineshop was in fact my spy."

I hadn't known, and I'd almost laughed out loud when the magus mentioned it outside the temple. The gods must have arranged it.

"I don't know how he would have gotten out of the prison on his own," said the magus. "It seems a foolhardy plan to have relied on my intervention."

I am a master of foolhardy plans, I thought. I have so much practice I consider them professional risks. Sooner or later they would have needed the cell and the chains for someone more important, the minister of the exchequer, for instance, and I would have been moved to another cell. Sooner or later I would have had my chance to escape, if I hadn't died of disease first.

"He couldn't have found the whereabouts of the stone from the papers in my study," the magus went on. "I was careful to destroy any records. But he could have followed us and stolen the Gift once it was located."

The minister of war snorted. "Not if he had to follow you on a horse," he said.

The queen laughed, and I flushed in the privacy of my bedroom. I do hate horses. That was the first sign that I wasn't going to be the soldier my father hoped for.

The magus might have heard me thinking. "He does have

other skills to be proud of," he said. For instance, I thought, stealing Hamiathes's Gift not once but twice. Who else in history had done that? But the magus referred to the fight with the Queen's Guard at the base of the mountain. That wasn't a skill I appreciated much. If I'd been as inept with a sword as I was in a saddle, my father might not have driven me so hard to be a soldier and to let the title of King's Thief lapse forever. It had been meaningless for so many generations, and he'd felt strongly that it should disappear for good.

The magus described the fighting with the guard in detail and made me look very good indeed.

The minister of war snorted. The magus didn't recognize this as high praise, and he said stiffly, "I've been told that his father wanted him to be a soldier. I'd be happy to inform his father that he has a son to be proud of."

I stifled a snort of my own in the silence that followed. The magus must have still been tired. He must have once known, but forgotten, that the minister of war had married the daughter of the previous King's Thief. He was talking to my father. The magus might have remembered this, might have recognized me from the first time he'd seen me in Sounis, but we had never been introduced. When he'd come with Sounis's marriage proposals, I had been sulking in my rooms.

While the magus, realizing his error, was trying to word an apology, my father came to look in at me. "I thought I heard you laughing up your sleeve," he said.

One arm was too tightly wrapped in bandages to move, but I held up the other to demonstrate that there was nothing up the sleeve of my nightshirt but my elbow.

"I'll come by later." Before he disappeared from the doorway, he nodded once, and that, I knew, would be his only sign of approval for all my hard work. He was not a man of many words.

After years spent trying to dissuade me from wasting my time acquiring valueless skills, he had come to my study one night to tell me why the queen of Eddis would consider a marriage proposal from Sounis and why her council, himself included, urged her to accept. He'd left a stack of double-heavy coins on the table and gone away.

A moment later the magus appeared in the doorway, closely followed by Sophos. "I'm glad to see you looking better," he said.

I looked at him out of the corner of my eye.

He smiled. "I've decided not to give you the satisfaction of gnashing my teeth." I laughed, while he looked around the room for a chair to sit in.

"That one is most comfortable." I lifted my hand out from under the sheets to point.

He sat down and put his feet up on a stack of books. We both remembered an earlier interview.

"I'll probably have to burn it," I said.

"Oh, no," he said. "I've had days to get clean."

"Days?" I said. Sophos was still hovering. "Push the books off the window seat," I told him, "and sit there. Has it really been days?"

"It has."

"What have I missed?"

"Not much," said the magus. "An emissary from the queen of Attolia, a few from Sounis—well, four from Sounis."

"Four?"

The magus shrugged one shoulder in an elegant gesture of boredom.

"Tell me," I said, "or I'll get up and strangle you with one hand. What did the messages say?"

"Oh, I believe that Attolia sends best wishes that the Queen's Thief is well and hopes that she will have a chance to entertain him for a longer period sometime in the future."

I grimaced at the thought.

"She knew who you were?"

"She must have strongly suspected. We'd only met very briefly, but she knows my reputation better than you did."

"She'll be plotting an elaborate revenge," said the magus.

"And you?"

"Am I planning an elaborate revenge? No, I haven't been able to think of anything adequate."

I laughed again. "I meant, did you suspect?"

The magus sighed. "No, not at all, at least not until you were able to make a bridge suddenly appear across the Seperchia. Then I started to think it wasn't an accident that I lost my way in the dark in the town. And I wondered if maybe the guards at the stone bridge recognized you. They seemed to have taken your appearance very much in stride. I wasn't certain until the captain welcomed me to Eddis—as if you belonged there and had brought Sophos and me as guests. That other bridge, did you know it would be there?"

"I go down every year after the floods have dropped and lodge a tree trunk there. My grandfather and I used to do it when he was alive. He liked to have a way to get into Attolia without being seen coming from Eddis."

"Pol knew," said Sophos from the window.

"Yes." The magus agreed. "When we watched you fighting with Sophos's sword, he whispered to me that you were Eddisian trained. I didn't understand what he was trying to tell me until later."

Pol had known before then, I was sure. He'd known from the moment I'd carelessly thanked him in my own words for the ossil berries. If he hadn't been pressed by the Attolians, and if he hadn't been so sure that the Gift had dropped in the stream, he wouldn't have let me out of his reach without searching me first.

The fact that he hadn't told the magus what he knew made

me think that he expected me to slip away once we were in the mountains and that he would have let me go. His orders were to keep Sophos safe and to bring back the Gift. Bringing back the Queen's Thief of Eddis hadn't been mentioned, I'm sure, and Pol must not have seen any reason to overreach his orders. I think he had liked me as much as I'd liked him.

"Ambiades might have guessed," I said. He and I had exchanged our information involuntarily beside the dystopia. I had realized that Ambiades was working for someone besides the magus, and he had realized that it would take one fraud to recognize another.

The magus shook his head. "Ambiades was clever. It's too bad he was a fool, too: always wanting more money, and more power . . . more respect. He would have made a fine magus if he could have stopped being the grandson of a duke."

For a moment we sat quietly thinking our own thoughts about ambition. I thought about Pol, who had seemed to be quite free of it, and I hoped he'd gotten some satisfaction pushing Ambiades over the edge of that cliff. All in all, I wished I could have done it myself.

Finally the magus said, "To think that I once beat the Queen's Thief with a horse crop."

I smiled and had to tell him that beating the Queen's Thief wasn't a rare honor.

"Oh? Is everyone on the mountain as skilled as you are with a sword?"

"Ah, but I don't use a sword." I explained that I hadn't held a sword in the two years since I'd torn up my enrollment papers in the Eddisian Guard. During an argument with my father I'd sworn, in front of an embarrassing number of people, not to take a sword by the hilt unless my life was in danger.

"Ah," said the magus, as if many things had grown more clear. I wondered whom he'd been talking to.

"You're tired," he said after a moment, and he was right. "We'll go."

"Wait," I said. "You haven't told me what Sounis said in his messages."

The magus shook his head. "You'll have to ask your queen that," he said. I followed his gaze to where the queen had been standing for I didn't know how long.

She was wearing a green shot silk dress that squeezed her under the arms and made her look like a peahen dressed up in her smaller husband's clothes. My brother Temenus had broken her nose with a practice sword when they were eleven, and the resulting bump had given her a comfortably settled plainness that was more attractive than all Attolia's beauty, but she didn't know that and often felt that she let her people down by not being more pretty. In her five-year reign she'd won the loyalty and love of her subjects. They thought she was beautiful, I told her, and they would be just as happy to see her in a sack as in the elaborate costumes her dressers liked to bully her into.

She twitched her lip at me to remind me that she felt she had a responsibility to be opulent if she couldn't be beautiful. I frowned because my good advice had obviously been forgotten while I'd been away.

The magus offered an apology for wandering away in the middle of their conversation, but she waved it aside, then sat on the bed beside me and squeezed my hand.

"I think you need more rest," she said.

"First I need to know what the emissaries from Sounis said."

"Eugenides, you're tired."

"I'll get up," I threatened, "and find someone else to tell me."

She gave in. I'd known she would. She wouldn't have come in and sat down otherwise.

"The first was just a stiff note to say that Sounis had removed his men from the forest on the southern slopes of Mount Irkes."

"He tried to sneak an army through the fir forest?"

"Yes."

"Aagh." I rolled my head back in contempt. "The idiot. See what he does when his magus isn't there to stop him? Did you set fire to the trees?"

The queen shook her head. "No, it wasn't necessary. I sent a note with your cousin Crodes telling him to get his men out by sunset or we'd burn the forest to the ground."

The magus's face paled at the thought of his country's entire army burnt to ash.

"The second emissary was more polite," the queen continued, settling back against my cushions. "The king of Sounis requested any information we had on the whereabouts and well-being of his magus and his heir."

"The magus's heir?" I asked.

"The king's heir."

I looked at Sophos. "Your father the duke is also the king's brother?"

"You didn't know?" he said.

"I did not."

The queen laughed. "With one move," she said, "you have secured my throne *and* brought me the heir of my enemy. The court is greatly impressed." It would be the first time for most of them, I thought. "I believe," she said, "I will extract a few concessions from Sounis before I send his nephew home."

She smiled at Sophos, and he blushed as he smiled back. She had that effect on most people, not just Sophos. A smile from her made anyone's blood warmer. There was good reason for the magus to want her as queen of his own country.

"But now it is time to go," the queen said, lifting herself off my cushions. She bent down to kiss my forehead as she freed her hand from mine, and I noticed Hamiathes's Gift swinging from the gold torque around her neck. As she stood, it settled back against her skin, just below her collarbones.

Two days later, long before I was ready to participate, there was an official ceremony to make my cousin Queen by Possession of Hamiathes's Gift. Evidently just handing her the stone didn't satisfy a lot of stuffy conventions. My father's dresser came and helped me struggle into fancy clothes. I wandered through the ceremony in a haze and managed a perfunctory appearance at the banquet afterward. My cousins made their usual thinly veiled insults. My aunts looked down their noses at me, and my uncles casually insulted me by remarking how *surprisingly* like my father I was turning out to be, as opposed to my mother's rather ne'er-do-well side of the family.

I couldn't seem to stir up any of my usual cutting comments in response. I was discreet, I suppose. Really, I didn't care, and I see now that it amounts to the same thing. I went to bed.

My fever climbed in the night, and my constant companions were the doctor and his assistants for the next week or so.

I remember the queen coming to me one night to offer me Hamiathes's Gift, but I told her I preferred to die. I'd had enough of Hamiathes's Gift and its rumored powers to confer immortality. There is something horrible and frightening and, I'd discovered, very, very painful about being trapped in this life when it is time to move on. She nodded wordlessly to me, as if she already understood. It may have been a dream.

When I finally felt better, I remained confined to my bed by the queen's physician. I had attended the ceremony against his vehement opposition, and he was feeling vindicated and authoritarian. He warned me that if I set a foot on the floor, he'd cut it off. I said that I thought the followers of Asklepios took an oath to do harm to no one. He said he'd make an exception for me.

Finally, negotiations had been settled between Sounis and Eddis, a new treaty had been drawn up, some compensation had been paid to the treasury of Eddis, and the magus and the king's heir were going home. They worked their way past the physician in order to say good-bye.

I sat myself up in bed as they came in.

"Magus"—I greeted him with a nod. "Your Highness"—I nodded to Sophos as well. He blushed.

"Was it because your mother was the Queen's Thief that you were called Eugenides?"

"Partly. It's closer to the truth to say that Eugenides is a family name and I was named after my grandfather. But my mother, you know, was never the Queen's Thief. She died before my grandfather did, and I inherited the title directly from him."

"But people called your mother Queen's Thief," said Sophos, puzzled. "At least, I've heard them say that."

I smiled. "She was a favorite at the court and was called Queen Thief, but not Queen's Thief. They said she stole people's hearts away. She certainly stole their jewels and wore them herself or sometimes dedicated them. She liked to take the things that people were most proud of. So if you flaunted your new emeralds, you were likely to see them next on Eugenides's altar, and once dedicated they were irretrievable. People were careful not to offend her." They'd learned not to offend me either.

Sophos started to say, "Your mother, did she—" and then stopped when he realized what he was asking.

"Fall out of a window when I was ten? Yes, but not out of

the Baron Eructhes's villa. She'd been dancing on the roof of the palace and slipped coming back in."

Sophos was quiet for a moment, looking for a safer subject. At last he blurted out, "When do you think you will get married?"

"I suppose it depends on when I find someone to marry," I said, puzzled.

"Well, you know." He floundered again.

I looked at him, perplexed. He was blushing. I looked at the magus to see if he knew what Sophos was hinting at, but he didn't. I finally had to ask, "Sophos, what do you mean?"

"Won't you marry the queen? Aren't you a favorite of hers, and isn't she queen because of you?"

"She's fond of me, Sophos, but that's because most of the rest of her cousins are morons. I'm very fond of her for the same reason, but I don't think I can make her queen and then insist she marry me as a return favor. The sovereign is *not* supposed to marry the thief. The possibility doesn't often arise and"—I hesitated as I watched the magus—"there are always political advantages to be considered when a sovereign marries." Eddis might still form an alliance with Sounis, although our queen would marry their king over my dead body.

"Gen—" Sophos started to ask another question, but I interrupted him.

"No," I said, "not Gen. Eugenides from now on. I never, never want to hear Gen again in my life."

The magus laughed while I shook my head.

"You haven't spent any time in the king's prison," I said. "And you haven't had to drink your way through every disreputable wineshop in the city of Sounis. I cannot tell you how sick I have been of cheap wine and of being dirty. Of talking with my mouth half closed and chewing with it open. Of having *bugs* in my hair and being surrounded by people who think Archimedes was the man at the circus last year who could balance four olives on his nose."

The magus looked around at the books piled in my study. "I remember that Archimedes. I think it was five olives," he said with a straight face.

"I don't care if it was twelve," I said.

The magus rubbed his hand across the carefully bound copy of the second volume of Archimedes. It was on top of the stack beside him. "You should have a few more modern writers," he said. "Eddis has been isolated too long. I'll send a few volumes with the next diplomatic party."

I thanked him, both of us thinking of the threat of the Medes. "Who will Sounis marry now?" I asked.

"I don't know," the magus admitted.

"You could always ask Attolia," I suggested.

He rolled his eyes and left, taking Sophos with him.

I was left to myself then, to luxuriate in my cotton sheets and to recover my strength. I made the reluctant physician bring me the books from my library to check the dating on the pillars outside the maze's entrance. They were unlike anything I could find recorded, and I came to believe that Hamiathes's Gift had been hidden in the temple under the Aracthus by every generation for hundreds of generations before the invaders had arrived on our shores and had been removed by each successive generation only with the gods' approval.

If you want to keep something safe from thieves, hide it carefully and keep a close watch over it.

My father visited often but briefly. On one visit he mentioned that Sophos had spent his days in the palace pointing out to one cousin after another that my tedious vow about handling a sword had been honorably retired. Several people did stop in to see me and to comment how much I had grown to look like my father, and not all of them seemed insincere. Maybe in the future my aunts and uncles would be willing to overlook the fact that I read too many books and can't ride a horse, sing a song in tune, or carry on polite conversation—all accomplishments that are supposed to be more highly valued than swordplay but aren't.

When the queen came by, she told me that the resemblance to my father was all in the way we both hunch over and then deny that we are in pain. I tried to insist that my shoulder didn't really bother me and it was time for me to be up. She laughed and went away.

After another week, when I was finally out of bed and resting in a chair, she came to visit and stayed longer than a minute or two. The evening sun was slipping around the shoulder of Hephestia's mountain and filling the room with orange light.

"Sophos went to see your family shrine to Eugenides," she said. "He admired all the earrings you've dedicated, particularly the duchess Alenia's cabochon emeralds." Someone must have told him how angry the duchess had been when I'd stolen them, so to speak, from under her nose. I suspected it was the queen.

I admitted that it was a little embarrassing to have him admire offerings to a god I hadn't previously believed in.

"I know," she said. We both looked at the Gift, turning over and over in her hands.

"Will you go on wearing it?" I asked.

"I couldn't stand it, I think," she said.

"Where will you put it if you take it off?" The temple was gone. It couldn't be returned there.

She was quiet for a long time. "I'm going to take it up to the sacred mountain and throw it into Hephestia's fire."

"You'll destroy it?" I was shocked.

"Yes. I'll take witnesses from here and from Sounis and Attolia as well, and when it is gone, Eddis's throne will descend in the same way as the thrones of other countries." She looked up at me. "Moira told me."

I nodded, remembering the messenger of the gods in her long white peplos.

"It wasn't meant to go on forever and ever," she said quietly. "It doesn't belong in this world."

"In a hundred years no one will believe it was real," I said. "But you'll still be famous."

"Oh, I don't know," I said. Lately fame had become a lot less important to me.

"Yes, you will," she said. "Because you're going to write it all down, and it will be a book in your library. But first you will tell me everything," she said. "The things the magus didn't know."

It was a relief to explain everything to her, to tell her about the prison and about the temple and what I'd thought of the magus in the beginning and what I thought of him in the end. What it meant to be the focus of the gods' attention, to be their instrument, used to change the shape of the world. And it was nice to brag a little, too.

It took me many days in the snatches of time she stole from royal functions and meetings with her ministers, but she wanted me to tell her everything, and I did. In the months since then, I have written it down. I will show it to her soon and see what she thinks. Maybe I will send a copy down to the magus.

*"So Sophos thinks you're going to marry me."*

*"While I think you'll marry Sophos."*

*"I might. We'll see what he's like when he grows up."*

*"I thought your council wanted you to marry that cousin of Attolia's?"*

*"No, that was just because he might have been better than Sounis. Now I needn't marry either. Which is fortunate for us all. They would have hated Eddis, but Sophos . . . I think Sophos might be happy here."*

"*Anyone lucky enough to be married to you would count his blessings.*"

"*Flatterer.*"

"*Not at all.*"

"*Eugenides . . .*"

"*Yes? Stop biting your lip, and say it.*"

"*Thank you, thief.*"

"*You're welcome, my queen.*"

# author's note

Nothing in this book is historically accurate, but I have taken bits and pieces out of the history of Greece and fitted them into my story. The landscape that Gen travels through is very much like that of ancient Greece and like some parts of modern Greece, as well. The gods he meets were never the gods of the Greek Pantheon. I made them up.

In the real world the bubonic plague traveled from somewhere east of the Black Sea in 1342 across all of Europe, killing millions. Gunpowder began to be used in cannons as early as 1339. Johann Gutenburg began printing books using movable type in 1445, and the pocket watch was invented in 1500.

2